The Dragonfly Delivery Company

KEITH W. DICKINSON

HAMMERSMYTH PRESS

Published by the Hammersmyth Press

GNU Terry Pratchett

Chapter 1

Something Must Be Done

Fluffy white clouds scudded beneath the airship's wooden hull, a moonlit layer of candyfloss atop the wine-dark sea of dirt below. They looked good enough to eat, like you could simply scoop some out of the air if you so desired. Stretching as far down as tip-toes would allow, Bert the cabin boy reached over the side to see if he could.

"Careful, young 'un," said the man at the helm. "It's a long way down if you go over."

Bert pulled back his hand. "I ain't goin' over. I knows what I'm doin'," he said testily.

The Helmsman laughed. "That's what they all say, and then slip, whoosh, arrgh, splat." Resting his chin on his hands, Bert stared out towards the horizon. "Anyway, it's about time you were off to bed, innit?" the Helmsman added. "It's getting late. We've got a full day of it tomorrow, y'know."

"But the captain said there'd be shooting stars tonight!" Bert protested. "I wants to see 'em." He would never admit it, but he had a particular wish that he wanted to come true.

"I don't care. I'm not having you fallin' asleep on the job coz you've been up all night."

"But I—"

"No buts, you little blighter. Bed, now!"

Sagging under the weight of every missed opportunity, Bert went below deck, mumbling a half-hearted goodnight to the Helmsman along the way. The Helmsman smiled. Young Bert was a good lad, even if he did have a bit of a mouth on him. He'd make a fine aeronaut one day.

Humming softly to himself, the Helmsman cast a weather eye over the ship's balloon before confirming once again that they were still on the right heading. It was a quiet night, with a steady wind. He didn't think he'd have anything to worry about. What he did have though was a gnawing feeling in the pit of his stomach. *Damn*, he thought. *I should have got Bert to bring me up some stew.* As if agreeing with him, his stomach gave a long, miserable groan.

Scanning the horizon for unexpected mountain ranges, the Helmsman tied off the wheel, before heading below deck to get himself something to eat.

Bert's head appeared through a hatch in the deck. Seeing the coast was clear, he scrambled up through the hole and hid behind a barrel, scanning the night sky intently as he crossed his fingers on both hands. He only needed to see one shooting star, just one, and he could go to bed happy, but as he swung his gaze from one horizon to the next all he saw was disappointment; disappointment as far as the eye could see. It looked like there'd be no new comic books for him the next time they came in to land.

Bert heard a thump. He turned, expecting a clip round the ear, and found a mushroom of metal hooks with a rope tied to it lying on its side in the middle of the deck. As he watched, the rope pulled taut, dragging the metal mushroom towards the side of the ship. Another bunch of hooks flew over the ship's rail, followed by a third, all three dragging across the deck until they caught on the railing and their ropes pulled tight. The ropes wiggled back and forth as one-by-one three figures climbed silently over the ship's rail. Unslinging the crossbows from their backs, they spread out across the deck, the three intruders making for the nearest hatch as they loaded their weapons.

Bert held his breath. *Sky pirates! Come to kill us all!* He had to warn the others.

As the three went below, Bert ran up onto the quarterdeck, where a brass bell hung next to the ship's wheel. "PIRATES! PIRATES!" he yelled, ringing the bell with all his might. "THERE'S PIRATES ON BOARD!" He grabbed the rope with both hands and rang it even harder. "WAKE UP! WAKE UP! THERE'S PIRATES ON THE SHIP!"

A dark figure loomed over Bert. He looked up into the eyes of certain death as he heard footsteps running down below.

The sky pirate brought his crossbow crashing down on top of Bert's head, knocking him to the ground. A thousand stars exploded before his eyes, none of them shooting (unfortunately). Stumbling to his feet, blood in his eyes, Bert ran for his life, staggering blindly across the quarterdeck straight towards the edge of the ship. Somewhere far away a familiar voice yelled, "NO!"

Bert's world turned upside down as he tipped over the quarterdeck's low rail, the wind whipping around him as he tumbled towards the fluffy clouds below. A hand reached out. A shooting star flew overhead. Following it with his eyes, Bert made one final, desperate wish.

"We have to do *something*!"

"We *are* doing something. We've changed the routes."

"It's not enough. We need to know how they know so much. We need an investigation."

"Pah! That'll never work. No one will talk."

"We have to try!"

"Why bother? It's a waste of time."

"*You're* a waste of time!"

"Come over here and say that!"

"Oh I will, you wait and see!"

"Well?"

"Well what?!"

"Well come on then!"

The Annual General Meeting of the Venerable Society of Airships Owners, Sky Captains, and Itinerant Washerwomen was going about as well as it usually did.

The teashop they'd rented for the occasion was jam-packed with aeronauts from both sides of the fence, be they the ones who paid the bills or the ones who did all the work, with a small group of washerwomen in the corner having themselves a nice cup of tea and a chinwag and staying well out of it. It was a lot of linen trousers, flouncy shirts, and wide-brimmed hats, against a wall of three-piece suits, pocket watches, and neatly trimmed beards, separated by a bundle of jolly, smiling, soapy-smelling women who looked like they could bend steel with just the force of their disapproving glare alone. The meeting used to be held in a local tavern until it became apparent that any access to alcohol was a recipe for disaster. Even now, at just gone eight in the morning, a few of the captains were already one-and-a-half sheets to the wind, which probably explained why the gathering was descending into chaos a mere five minutes after it had been called to order.

Fortescue Frobisher, chairman of the society, breathed a heavy sigh. He didn't need this today. Pushing himself wearily to his feet, he removed his shoe and banged it loudly on the tabletop, rattling the teapots. "That's enough! Everybody settle down. This is no way to conduct business. Captain Lewis, let go of Mr Hargreaves at once! Thank you. Now, gentlemen,"—one of the washerwomen gave a discreet cough—"and ladies, despite our differences I think we can all agree that this situation cannot be allowed to continue. These so-called sky pirates have been taking a considerable slice of our collective pie for far too long now. They need to be stopped, and I have the solution." He held up a newspaper for everyone to see. A captain in the front row squinted up at the headline.

"You want to throw a tea party for all the maids in the city?"

"What? No. Not that." The chairman pointed to a small, blurry photograph of a man and a cat at the bottom of the page. "This."

The captain in the front row read the headline next to the picture. "Is this the world's richest cat?"

"Oh for heaven's sake, not the cat. The man next to it. That is John Sinister, the man who found Donald Chard's killer. If anyone can figure out what's going on, I'm sure he can."

That got a murmur of approval from everyone, even the washerwomen. Donald Chard was a legend in the aeronautic world, a hero to them all. The father of modern aeronautics, his loss had been keenly felt, and whilst having his killers behind bars was scant solace for the lack of his indomitable presence, it seemed reasonable to assume that anyone who had done right by Donald Chard would do right by them as well.

"Oh yeah?" said Captain Lewis, the man responsible for rumpling Mr Hargreaves. "And who's going to pay for all this? I'm sure a man like that ain't gonna come cheap."

"I'll pay for it out of my own pocket if I have to," said the chairman. "Although I'm sure we have enough in the coffers to cover such an investigation." He glanced at the bursar who nodded hastily.

The airship owners present seemed to like this idea very much. Their captains less so.

"Yeah, right," said Captain Lewis. "And who's going to carry him, eh? If I bring a spy on board me lads'll go nuts. They don't like having no strangers about, believe me. He's apt to get chucked overboard afore we reach the outskirts, you mark my words."

There was a chorus of agreement from the rest of the captains. They hadn't become air couriers because they liked people poking their nose into their business. There was a fine line between courier work and smuggling, a line many of them danced on a daily basis like they were doing a highland fling.

"I will take him," said a voice from the back of the room. The collected captains all turned as one.

Sitting with her feet up on a table, the brim of her feathered hat pulled down low, the lounging figure looked to be asleep but for the cup and saucer she had balanced in front of her. Tilting her head back just enough, she considered all the unwashed faces looking back at her. "I have no problem taking someone on board. *My* crew do what they are told, if they know what is good for them."

"But of course," barked Captain Lewis. "It'd be just like a woman to—"

There was a sudden squeak of chairs and the room fell silent. Captain Lewis turned slowly to find all of the assembled washerwomen giving him their *full* attention. Some of them were clutching knives, some of them tiny forks, and none of them were smiling. One was even brandishing a particularly spiky-looking rock bun like she knew how to use it, and whilst Captain Lewis didn't know what she was planning on doing with it, he was quite certain that he didn't want it happening to him.

"Enough," said the chairman. "Mrs Trowbury, put that chair down. Mrs Glossop, put that cake stand back where you found it at once! There's an easy way to settle this. We can take a vote."

An approving murmur went round the room. The captains liked this idea. There was safety in numbers. No one could make them back something if they didn't want to. If they all voted no what could anyone do? The motion didn't stand a chance. But as they glanced at Mrs Trowbury, who still hadn't put that chair down, they soon realised that this was not going to be what you might call a 'free' vote in the more traditional sense of the word.

John Sinister, Hammersmyth's most famous detecting agent (being the only one anyone had ever heard of) walked down a cobbled side street, his not-so-silent partner in their newly-minted detecting agency trotting along beside him. Dexter was the world's only walking, talking, mechanical cat. The most advanced automaton in the Britannic Empire, only two people knew of his existence – John Sinister, and his Japanese creator, Nomko. But now the time had come to let someone else in on their little secret, and Dexter for one couldn't wait to see how he would react.

"What do you think he'll do?" he said, grinning. "Do you think he'll faint? I think he'll faint."

"He's not going to faint."

"But he might do though, eh? I mean, you never know."

"He might, but I doubt it. He doesn't seem the fainting type."

"What, then? Will he swear, do you think? Fall off his chair? Something like that."

"From what I know of Mr Holberton, I think you'll be lucky to get a raised eyebrow."

"A raised eyebrow? A cat starts talking to him and you think all I'll get is a raised eyebrow? Be serious."

"I am being serious. He doesn't strike me as the kind to rattle easily. I think a raised eyebrow is all you're going to get."

"Nah. I think you're wrong. I think he'll faint."

Charles Holberton QC stared at the grey tortoiseshell tabby sitting in the chair opposite. In his nearly forty years before the bar he thought he'd seen every type of client there was, from the desperate, to the delusional, to the downright insane, but this was a new one on him. It just went to show, when you started making assumptions you made an ass out of you and umptions.

"Goodness me," he said. The cat chuckled.

"You were right," it said. "Not even a raised eyebrow."

John Sinister shrugged. "Told you. The man's unflappable."

"Well I wouldn't go that far," said Mr Holberton, his eyes still firmly fixed on Dexter. He sat forward, leaning on his desk. "You're an automaton, you say? Built by Chard Mechanical?"

"That I am."

"Fully independent? Capable of independent thought?"

"As much as either one of you, and probably more than this numpty," said Dexter, nodding towards John with a sly smirk.

"Well I never," said Mr Holberton, sitting back in his chair once more.

The past couple of weeks had been amongst the most bizarre the firm of Holberton, Hutchison, and Murphy had ever known. Not only had their biggest client, Donald Chard, the richest and most famous industrialist in the Britannic Empire, died in the very office in which they now sat, not only had said client chosen to leave his not-inconsiderable estate to the family cat, but now it seemed that the cat in question wasn't a cat at all, but was in fact an automaton, and quite the most advanced automaton the world had ever known. As previously stated, a bizarre couple of weeks indeed.

"Although I must say," Mr Holberton continued, "this revelation does shed light on some of the more unusual stipulations in Mr Chard's will."

"Such as?" asked John.

"Well, there's the emancipation proclamation for a start. Mr Chard left instructions that upon his death the cat known as Dexter was to be declared legally independent, something which I confess initially confounded me. Why would a cat need to be declared free from ownership? But now I understand. Without the declaration, Dexter would have remained the property of Chard Mechanical, and as such would have been unable to inherit the company. One cannot own property if you yourself are owned by said property."

"So... I *am* the new owner of Chard Mechanical then?" asked Dexter.

Mr Holberton scrunched up his face. "Not exactly. You see, whilst you can be declared not property, you cannot be declared a person within the law, and so cannot own anything. Chard Mechanical has been placed into a trust, which will be managed on your behalf."

"And who manages the trust?"

"Normally a trustee would have been stipulated in the will, but in this case the trustee is to be determined. Actually, the will states that the beneficiary, i.e. you, must appoint a trustee of their own choosing, a situation I had no idea how we were going to resolve until now."

"So I own everything, but I have to choose someone to speak for me, is that it?"

"Exactly."

"Will you do it?"

Mr Holberton chuckled. "Good Lord, no. As the executor of the will, and as legal counsel to the Chard estate, for me to insert myself into the middle of all this would be unwise to say the least. No, I suggest you appoint someone you trust to act as your mouthpiece. Someone who can act on your behalf, but who is unlikely to rip you off the first chance they get."

Dexter and Mr Holberton both turned to look at John, who suddenly felt his world get a lot more complicated. "Oh, come on! I don't want to run some massive company. Can you imagine what a pain that would be?"

"You wouldn't have to run anything, Mr Sinister. The general manager would do that for you. This would just be to keep all the paperwork nice and neat. Although, the two of you *will* have to find a new general manager to run things on Mr Dexter's behalf, seeing as how everyone who was previously eligible to run the company is now either dead or in jail."

"And how do we go about doing that?"

"I have no idea, but I suggest you do so sooner rather than later. Chard Mechanical is in a bit of a mess, to say the least. She needs a firm hand on the tiller before the whole thing goes up in smoke, if you catch my drift."

There was a knock at the door and Mr Holberton's clerk entered, a sour look on his already sour face. Through the door, the incessant yapping of a frantic, highly-agitated dog could be heard coming from downstairs. The company dog, Liebling, a bad-tempered, wire-haired terrier, had been locked in a cupboard for the duration of Dexter's visit, and neither he nor Mr Wilberforce were too pleased about the fact.

"A message from Chard Manor, sir, via the radiophone. For the… gentleman."

John was impressed. Much like on his first visit to the offices of Holberton, Hutchison, and Murphy, the clerk had managed to pack more contempt into the word 'gentleman' than John would ever have thought possible.

He read the message. "Well would you look at that," he said. "It seems we have another case."

In a not very large clearing full of dappled sunlight and the sounds of summer, a black airship hung from the trees at a funny angle, its nose tipped close to the ground like it had stumbled on its way through the forest and was still in the process of falling over. Its balloon, horribly deflated, was entangled among the treetops, pierced in several places in what even the most casual observer could see was an extremely unplanned landing.

Two men walked around the suspended ship, the one in carpenter's overalls sucking on his teeth and shaking his head as he assessed the damage, whilst the other, dressed all in black with a badly-painted skull on his chest, watched on in anxious trepidation.

The man in the overalls crouched down to look underneath the ship. "Dear oh dear," he said, tutting. "Oh deary, deary me. What a mess."

"Well?" said the other man, wringing his hands. "Can it be fixed?"

The first man pushed himself upright, wincing at the pain in his knees. He was too old to be out in the woods this early. Repairing pirate ships was a young man's game. "Fixed? Of course she can be fixed. That's not the problem. The question is, is she worth fixing?"

"What do you mean?"

"Well…" said the carpenter, pausing for dramatic effect.

A donkey that had seen more than its fair share of disappointment appeared on the edge of the clearing, bearing an absolute giant of a man as though such a burden was to be expected from a world as cold and cruel as this one. The man was all muscle and sinew, his scarred torso barely covered by a filthy sheepskin waistcoat. His hands were like sledge hammers, his neck was thicker than his head, and his gaze flitted around the clearing like a hunter searching for its prey.

The young man with the skull on his chest straightened up, swallowing nervously.

The giant took his time dismounting, confident that the world would wait for him. He didn't bother tying the donkey to a tree, it wasn't going anywhere. "Well?" the man said, taking in the battered airship.

"Well," said the carpenter, skipping the dramatic pause this time, "as I was sayin', I can fix her up for you no problem, the question is, is it worth it? The way she is at the moment you'd almost be better off scrapping her and buying a new one."

"Why? She doesn't look that bad to me."

The carpenter crouched down low, beckoning the other two men to join him. He pointed underneath the ship, where the spine of its keel rested heavily on a very large rock. "You see there, where she's hit the ground? You see the crack in the wood? The impact broke her back. That'll need shoring up afore she can go anywhere, although to be safe I'd recommend replacing the main beam altogether."

"That sounds like a big job," said the giant.

"Oh it is. And expensive. Like I say, you'd be better off buying a new ship and using this one for spare parts."

The three men stood. "I take it there's no way of getting her out of here and back to the cavern?"

The carpenter shook his head. "Not that I can see, no."

"Could we patch up the balloon and fly her out?"

"Not unless you want her breaking in half mid-flight."

The giant gave an angry sigh. He glared at the man in black who took an instinctive step backwards. Turning abruptly, the giant strode over to the waiting donkey. "Thank you for your time, Mr Grimes, but I don't think we'll be needing your services today."

"Right you are, guv," said the carpenter, annoyed, but smart enough to keep that to himself.

"But what about the ship?" said the man in black. "What do you want me to do with her?"

The giant climbed back astride the poor donkey, the animal staggering slightly under his considerable weight. He turned to face the two men. "Burn it," he hissed. "Burn it all."

John and Dexter arrived at Mrs Muggins' Teashop to be greeted by a scene of utter dining devastation. Whoever had been in there that morning seemed to have eaten everything they could lay their hands on, had a food fight with what was left, had a massive argument over who would pay the bill, then done a runner. Every table was strewn with dirty dishes and unused napkins, save for the one in the corner where all the plates had been licked clean and piled neatly, ready for collection. A lone waitress went about the place, a grim look on her face, trying to make a dent on the carnage as she seriously reconsidered her life choices thus far.

A man of obvious means stood by the fireplace, talking to a Japanese woman sat in a leather armchair who, as far as John was concerned, couldn't have looked any more louche if she tried. She was dressed like a musketeer from that book they made John read at school, complete with knee-high leather boots, a frilly white shirt with actual flounces down the front, and a bandolier across her chest that ended in a short but very lethal-looking sword hanging at her right hip. Sat with one arm thrown casually over the back of her chair, she clearly had no interest in what was being discussed, and was feigning it simply to be polite.

"Hey! I hope that thing's house trained," said the maid, pointing at Dexter.

"Oh, don't worry. He won't make a mess, will you, boy?" said John.

Dexter shook his head, smiling innocently at the maid. Then he caught himself. "Er… meow?" he said, doing his best to look like a normal, average, everyday cat. The maid didn't care. She'd already gone back to her tidying up.

Seeing John enter, the man of means hurried over, his hand extended. "Mr Sinister. Thank you for coming. You got my message then?"

"Indeed, Mr Frobisher. A pleasure to make your acquaintance. Now tell me, what can I do for the Air Couriers Guild?"

Mr Frobisher beckoned John over to the fireplace. "For a number of years our members have been dealing with a growing scourge that has become a real blight on our livelihoods. It is this scourge that I am hoping you can help me with." John stared blankly at Mr

Frobisher. "I'm talking about piracy, Mr Sinister. Thieving. Good, old-fashioned, robbery with menaces."

"Piracy! On an airship? Is that even possible?"

"Very much so, and whilst a certain amount of loss is to be expected in our line of work, recently it has gotten much, much worse. It used to be all harpoons on hilltops and attacks whenever we came in to land, problems that were, to a certain extent, avoidable. But then six months ago these sky pirates went and got themselves a couple of airships of their own. Ever since then our losses have tripled, with some of our members going out of business altogether. As I say, they have become a real blight on business, one which we must do something about."

"You have my sympathies, sir, but I don't see how I can help. I can't fight a bunch of pirates for you."

"And I'm not asking you to. Fighting is not the issue. Our crews can hold their own against these blackguards, although Lord knows they shouldn't have to. No, the problem is with how well informed they are. These sky pirates seem to know our every move. They know when to strike, where to strike, and who is carrying the most valuable cargo."

"So you want me to find out how they know so much? Where they're getting their information from?"

"Exactly," said Mr Frobisher

John thought for a moment. "I can do that, probably, although I confess I'm not sure where to start with something like that."

Mr Frobisher gestured at the woman in the comfy chair. "Captain Tonbo here is about to go on a run right through the heart of their territory." John turned towards the louche musketeer who gave him a brief nod. "She has agreed to take you on board as crew, so that you can see first-hand what the situation is. Hopefully you will observe something along the way that will prove of use."

"On board an airship you mean?"

"Is that a problem?"

Plummeting to my death from a thousand feet? thought John. *No, no problem at all.* "It's fine," he said. "Although taking on a job so hazardous will affect my fee somewhat."

"How much are we talking about?" said Mr Frobisher.

"Five pounds a day," said John, plucking a number from thin air.

"Preposterous. There's no way the guild can afford that. Five pounds a week, maybe."

"Make it ten pounds a week and you've got a deal."

"I tell you what," said Mr Frobisher. "If you can figure it out in a week we'll pay you ten pounds. If not, we'll pay you five, and five pounds the week after, depending on if you're making progress or not. Deal?"

"Deal."

"Excellent. Now, if you will excuse me, I'll leave you in the capable hands of Captain Tonbo. Good day, Mr Sinister. And good luck." Shaking John's hand, Mr Frobisher left.

Turning to address Captain Tonbo, John noticed for the first time that her right arm was mechanical, a fairly functional prosthesis that looked like it extended all the way up to the elbow. That explained why she kept her sword on her right hip. Although the hand looked well made, it probably lacked the dexterity required for moments of sword fighting, swashbuckling, and general derring-do. "Well? Where do we begin?"

The captain considered John for a very long time. Standing, she grabbed a grey greatcoat from over the back of her chair and swung it over her shoulders with an impressively well-practised flourish. "Are you familiar with Ship Fields?"

"I am," said John, as the captain donned an expensive-looking black hat with a red ostrich feather tucked into its band.

"Good. You and your partner be there at eleven sharp. And dress warm. It gets cold up high, even on a nice day like this."

"I'm sorry, my partner?"

"Your partner, yes. Mr Frobisher said there would be two of you. You are Dexter *and* Sinister, Detecting Agents, are you not?"

John glanced at Dexter, who gave him a 'don't ask me what to do' look. "Of course. My partner, yes. Absolutely. We'll be there. No problem whatsoever."

"This is a problem," said John, as he and Dexter crossed the bridge into Barns Tenements.

"Why? Just tell 'em I'm your partner. Problem solved."

"Yeah, right. 'Hello. This is Dexter, the talking cat. He's a detecting agent, just like me!' They'd lock me up and throw away the key."

"Alright, so don't tell them I can talk, then."

"That's not the part they'd lock me up for."

They turned onto the street of washed-out tenements where his sister lived. A trio of small boys who gave the term grubby a bad name were playing football against a wall, whilst on the other side of the road two young women in housecoats, with a baby on one hip and a basket of washing on the other, were busy putting the world to rights.

Dexter clammed up as they walked past the women, John nodding his hellos in that 'I've seen you around and I know we know people in common so that makes us acquaintances even though we've never been properly introduced' way that was a cornerstone of tenement life. He was going to nod to the kids too, but they were too busy playing football to pay him no nevermind, which is just as it should be.

John had been living in the tenements for over a year, and whilst he had now 'officially' moved into one of the spare bedrooms at Chard Manor, the massive country house that Dexter had recently inherited, he'd been taking his sweet time about the actual move. All his stuff may have been packed in a dozen scrounged boxes and bags, but it was still taking up space in his sister's living room.

John found an unexpected tandem bike leaning against the wall outside his sister's house. Keeping an eye on it was his niece, Emily. She had a lace tutu on over her normal everyday clothes, and was leaping about throwing kicks into the air. This surprised John more than the bike, as Emily was not your average, tutu-wearing kind of a girl.

"Alright, Em? What you up to?"

"Combat ballet," said Emily, a stern look of concentration on her face. "So I can defend myself against the cannibals."

John looked around. "What cannibals?"

"For when I go exploring! All the adventurers do it, an' I'm gonna be a proper adventurer when I grows up."

"Good thinking," said John. "Always smart to plan ahead." Emily did an extra hard air-kick and her shoe fell off. She went into the gutter to retrieve it. "Say, Emily, can you keep an eye on Dexter for me whilst I go and talk to your mum? You know how he hates being left on his own."

"Yay!" said Emily, scooping Dexter up in her arms. Sitting down on the kerb, she hugged him tight as she buried her face in his fur. Dexter glared after John as he went inside, maintaining his indignation as long as he could before eventually giving in to the cuddles that he, like all those who pride themselves on their toughness, secretly craved.

John found his sister, Jane, in the kitchen with her new best friend, Agnes Goodenough. Agnes was Nigerian by birth and Cock-a-knee by nature. The head bouncer down at Caesar's Coffee And Chocolate Emporium – which was neither a coffee shop, an emporium, nor run by a guy named Caesar – she was the living embodiment of the phrase 'You and whose army?' Agnes had been instrumental in helping John solve his last case. She'd also been instrumental in saving his sister's life, redefining everyone's idea of what a right good kicking looked like along the way. There was a large red stain on the pavement by the front door from where she'd dealt with one of the men that had been sent to hurt Jane, and it was rumoured the other one would be walking with a limp for the rest of his born days.

Agnes was as impressive and intimidating as a falling oak, which was why the dance she and Jane did as they moved around the kitchen was so unexpected. They moved about the small room with familiar ease, warning one another of their presence with a gentle touch of the hip or a hand laid lightly on the small of the back.

"Morning, you two," said John, leaning in the doorway of the kitchen.

Jane smiled. "Morning, John."

"Sinister," said Agnes, with a curt nod.

"What's all this then?"

"Agnes and I are going on a picnic."

"Yeah. We're gonna go up Paradise Hill and watch the airships turning round," said Agnes.

"Agnes loves her some airships," said Jane, smiling at the woman by her side.

Jane and Agnes had been inseparable over the past couple of weeks, going to tea tastings, art galleries, all-female poetry nights, that kind of thing. They'd even had dinner at Le Petit Mort, a high-end restaurant in the fancy part of town, which John wouldn't have thought either one of them would be into. "Treating yourselves, eh?"

"Damn right," said Agnes. "It's about time our Jane here had a proper day off. She deserves it, wouldn't you say?"

"Indeed I would," said John, grinning at his sister.

Jane looked away, playing nervously with a thumb ring John had never seen her wear before. She never had been comfortable with such compliments.

A thought occurred to John. "Say, Agnes, how are you fixed work-wise for the rest of the week?"

Agnes stopped making sandwiches to squint suspiciously at John. "I'll be on the door at Caesar's, as per. Why?"

"It's just I've got this job on see, and I thought maybe—"

"Let me stop you right there," said Agnes, brandishing a buttery knife. "Last time I worked for you I nearly got meself killed, and that is not a mistake I intend on making twice in one lifetime. So thanks, but no thanks. Besides, I've promised your sister a proper day out, and I intend to keep my promise. Got it?" She went back to buttering four thick slices of bread.

"Yeah, you're probably right," said John, coming over all non-chalant. "Besides, crewing an airship ain't for everyone."

Agnes's head jerked up. "Crewing a what now?!"

John inspected his fingernails with extreme interest. "An airship. I've got a job working with the Air Couriers Guild. It'd mean flying up and down the country for a few days seeing if we can't figure out how come they keep getting robbed." He gave Agnes a look of pure innocence. "That's not something you'd be interested in, is it?"

Agnes bit her lip. She turned to Jane as if expecting trouble but Jane merely laughed. "Oh go on, you big softie. You two have fun."

"Are you sure? You're not disappointed?"

"Of course I'm disappointed, but I'm not gonna stand between you and a ride in an airship, now am I? That really would be sad. We can always go on our bike ride another time. Paradise Hill's not going anywhere."

"Thank you, Jane. You're the best," said Agnes, squeezing Jane's hand.

Jane smiled up at Agnes, taking a half step towards her before shooting her brother a quick sideways glance. Hurriedly smoothing down her apron, she quickly found something else for her hands to do.

In the far, far north of England, in a land of long lakes and rocky mountains, a young woman in distinctly piratey garb (lots of hard-wearing leathers and dark, tough cottons) sat on a grassy hillock watching a steady stream of smoke emerge from the middle of a small wood several large hillsides away.

A young man came up the hill to join her. "What are you looking at?" he asked, following her gaze.

She pointed towards the smoke. "That's where the *Dauntless* went down."

"Do we know what happened yet?"

"Toby and his boys screwed up again."

"Skull."

"What?"

"He's calling himself Skull these days."

The young woman shook her head. "Of course he is."

The two watched the smoke for a while, the wispy white turning a thick dark grey whenever the flames below found something they could really sink their teeth into.

"Right. We should get ready," said the woman, standing.

"Ready? Ready for what?"

"We're about to get a visit from Fenris."

"We are?"

"We are."

"Why?"

The woman headed off back down the hill. "Because he's about to make us an offer we can't refuse, and he's not going to like it when we do."

Chapter 2

The Dragonfly Takes Flight

There were two types of airship in the world. There were the huge transatlantic air liners, with their yacht-like gondolas and gleaming white balloons, that plied their trade high above the ocean waves, their passengers enjoying endless cocktails as they snacked on tiny canapés, safe in the knowledge that they were well-to-do and everybody knew it. And then there were the slap-dash, make-do, built from whatever they could lay their hands on, air couriers. Made from the hulls of old sailing ships slung beneath patchy misshapen balloons, held together by steel-laced twine and extra-strength horse glue, the folks aboard these makeshift beauties knew their place in the world too, only they were a darn sight less happy about it.

The cruise ships of the Air Line flew out of a purpose-built facility to the west of Hammersmyth, a modern, glass and iron building full of fancy restaurants, comfy chairs, and splinter-free toilet seats. The ramshackle fleet of air couriers flew from a muddy hill to the south of town, just past the forges along the river, where tying your ship to a stake in the ground cost you nothing at all. There was a wooden hut that served tea and biscuits, run by a sweet old lady who didn't mind if your feet were mucky, and there was even a small toilet block and shower if you were feeling brave (and had become very adept at breathing through your ears).

John was still amazed at the strange twist of fate that had led to Dexter now owning the Transatlantic Air Line. He'd have been jealous if he didn't know how monumentally in debt it all was. The whole thing operated on a wing and a prayer, more so than any of the air couriers tethered to the hill up ahead. He was glad it was somebody else's job to sort that mess out. Unfortunately it appeared to be his job to find that somebody else.

John trudged up the hill known as Ship Fields, Dexter trotting along beside him. He was a bit warm in his heavy winter coat (a scratchy woollen item bought more for its ability to double as a blanket if necessary than anything else) but if it was as cold up there as Captain Tonbo had intimated he'd be glad of it soon enough. He saw Agnes waiting for him at the top of the hill. She too looked a little flushed in her thick black suit and heavy black over-coat, but she obviously wasn't about to let that dampen her enthu-siasm. She could barely contain her excitement at being around so many airships, let alone the prospect of having a ride in one.

"I see Nero gave you the time off then," said John.

"I told you he would, din' I," said Agnes. "Besides, it's not like I left him in the lurch. I got my mate Lionel to fill in for me." Agnes grinned. "You remember Lionel, don't you, Sinister."

John did. He had met Lionel – a giant of a man so big he made Agnes look positively average – exactly twice, and both times the man had tried to kill him. Not that his heart had been in it, you understand, he'd been on the job both times, but still, it did put a bit of a dampener on their relationship. The only thing John liked about Lionel was the fact that he wasn't there right now. "How could I forget," he said. "Let's hope he doesn't kill any of the regulars before you get back."

Agnes dismissed the idea with a wave of her hand. "He'll be fine. He's a smart lad. So long as everyone behaves themselves they'll have nothing to worry about. Anyway, enough of that. Which one of these is us then?"

John considered the three airships tied up at the top of the hill. The two nearest were large stubby vessels with thick hulls and round, oval balloons. Old ships of the line that had been stripped to their bare bones before being put back into service, they both had large propellers sticking out their back ends, connected no doubt to a very large, very hungry engine within. Neither was what you might call elegant, or efficient, or even up to snuff, but they did look like they could take whatever the world threw at them and still come out the other side (and in fact probably had) so they had that going for them at least.

Compared to the other two, the third ship looked positively made to order. Built from the hull of an old tea cutter, her front end had two glass observation domes either side of her forecastle, whilst her quarter deck had been elongated out the back giving her a rather impressive looking tail. Long and sleek and well maintained, there were no missing uprights in any of *its* railings, and if any of *its* boards had been replaced they had been sanded flat and stained to match as well.

Her balloon was long and sleek too. Pointed at both ends, it was attached to the hull by a neat web of rigging that would make a sailor's mother proud, although that wasn't the most impressive thing about her. That honour went to the two sets of sails that jutted out either side of the ship, long wing-like loops of wood and sheer canvas which, as much as her two glass 'eyes', told John that this was the ship they were looking for. "Well, Captain Tonbo said her ship was called the *Dragonfly*, so I'm guessing that's the one we want."

"Really?!" said Agnes, her eyes lighting up. "Are you sure?"

"You see any other ships that look like a dragonfly around here?"

John, Agnes, and Dexter headed over. They saw Captain Tonbo on the deck of the ship, arguing with one of her crew; a quiet, furious argument the kind in which no one is willing to back down even if the other one is right. With a sharp wave of her hand, the captain ended the debate, and the man stormed off muttering under his breath. She turned to the rail to take a moment and saw John and Agnes looking up at her. Standing up straight and adjusting her hat, she headed down the steep gangplank to greet them.

The captain had gotten rid of all the fancy clothes she'd had on earlier. Dressed in a sturdy pair of boots, some loose dark cotton trousers, a cable-knit sweater, and a leather tricorn hat, she looked ready to go to work. All that other stuff must have been for show, dressing up to impress the other captains. Only the greatcoat remained, which came as no surprise to John. Such a reliable item of clothing probably went with her everywhere.

"Mr Sinister. About time. We are ready to cast off. This must be your associate? Miss Dexter, I assume. Or is it Mrs?"

"It's miss actually, Captain," said John quickly. "Miss Agnes Dexter. Agnes, this is Captain Tonbo."

Agnes glanced sideways at John. She held out her hand. "Pleased to meet you, Captain. And might I say what a fine ship you have. Never have I seen the like."

"Thank you. Yes, she is a beauty, is she not? The *Dragonfly* is my pride and joy. You will not find faster, Miss Dexter, I guarantee it."

"She's rather unusual, if you don't mind me saying. How does she make way?"

"With her sails," said the captain, pointing out the two sets of wings. "With these she needs neither engine nor propellor, just a steady wind and a firm hand on the wheel. She will outstrip any of these other barges before they have even gotten up a head of steam."

"Of that I have no doubt," said Agnes, admiring the ship alongside Captain Tonbo.

John knew better than to interrupt two people having a moment. Dexter, unfortunately, didn't. He cleared his throat loudly. The captain looked down. "Is that your cat?" she said, watching Dexter closely.

"It is, yes. He'll be coming with us. I, er, wasn't able to find anyone to take care of him at such short notice. I hope that's okay?"

"It will have to be, I suppose. Just keep him under control and away from the kitchen. If the cook catches him stealing food there is no telling what he will do."

"Not a problem. He'll behave himself, won't you, Dexter?"

"Meow," said Dexter, smiling.

The captain frowned. "Your cat is called Dexter too, as well as your associate? That is a little unusual, do you not think?"

John's mouth moved up and down. No sounds came out.

"Purely a coincidence," said Agnes. "We laughed about it when we found out, didn't we, John?" John nodded dumbly.

The captain seemed unimpressed.

"If you will make your way on board we can get under way."

Captain Tonbo went back up the gangplank. John was about to follow her when he felt a massive hand grab him by the elbow.

"When were you going to fill me in on my new name?" hissed Agnes.

"Uh, yeah. Sorry about that. Slipped my mind. But they were expecting two people, and I couldn't tell them the other half of my agency was just a name on a letterhead, now could I? I mean, how would that have looked? You understand, don't you?"

"Listen, I've got no problem pulling a fast one, been doing it all my life, but you've got to give me a heads up beforehand, right? Otherwise I'm apt to give the whole game away."

"Got it," said John, glancing at Dexter as he trotted up the gangplank. "No more secrets from now on."

Captain Tonbo was waiting for them on the deck of the *Dragonfly*, standing next to the crewman she'd been having an argument with earlier.

"This is our engineer, Mr Watson."

"I still think this is a bad idea," the man mumbled. Captain Tonbo silenced him with a hard look. With great reluctance, he shook hands with John and Agnes. "Michael Watson, at your service. But please, call me Mick."

"Pleased to meet you, Mick," said John, taking in the man's unusual clothes. Either he liked shopping at the army surplus store or he was ex-military, possibly infantry, although it was hard to tell since all his things had been stripped of their insignia. He was quite obviously an engineer though. His sleeves were rolled up, his forearms were greasy, and he had a filthy rag and spanner hanging out his back pocket.

"Michael is the only one on board who knows who you really are and why you are here. If I am not around, and you need help with anything, you can speak with him. He knows the ship better than I do, and he knows the air courier business like the back of his hand."

Mick looked away, uncomfortable with all the attention. "I needs to be getting on," he mumbled, disappearing below deck as fast as he could. *Yup, definitely an engineer,* thought John.

The captain sighed, shaking her head. At the far end of the deck a small door opened and another man appeared. "Ah, Mr Jackson. A moment, if you please."

The man caught sight of John and Agnes and his face sank. He clomped over, his jaw clenched, caught in a tug of war between being respectful to the captain and a lot of unhappy swearing. "Ma'am," he said, tugging at his forelock.

"Mr Jackson, these are our two new recruits. Miss Dexter and Mr Sinister. Miss Dexter is here to help us see off any sky pirates that might happen our way, and Mr Sinister has come to replace Bert, since he is no longer with us."

"Bit old fer a cabin boy, in'ne?"

"Nevertheless, that is the case. Will you see that they get squared away, then assign them their duties?"

Mr Jackson sighed. "Aye, Captain," he said wearily, the weight of the world on his shoulders.

"Good man. We cast off in five minutes. Prepare to weigh anchor."

"Very good, ma'am," Mr Jackson replied, tugging on his forelock once more.

The captain left them to it. Mr Jackson waited for her to get out of earshot, which John foolishly took to mean it was his turn to speak. "Pleased to meet you, Mr Jackson, I—"

"Alright, that's enough out of you." Jackson growled. "I dunno where the captain found you two, but I'm guessing it wasn't down no shipyard. I mean, look at the state of ya! I 'ope you're not attached to them fancy-shmancy clothes of yours, coz they'll not last two minutes round here. Can either of you tie a knot? No, of course you can't. I dunno why I'm even askin'. Look, just do what I say when I say and you might last the week, if you're lucky. And there'll be no more of this Mr Jackson nonsense, neither. I works for a livin'. The name's Jacko. I'm the bosun round here, I runs the ship, and what I say goes, got it?"

"Sure thing," said John.

"You're the boss, boss," said Agnes.

Jacko turned to leave, but then he turned back again. "Oh, and one last thing." He pointed at the balloon above their heads. "I 'ope neither one of you smokes, coz that thing there wants nothing more than to explode, so if I sees either one of you with a pipe, a cigar, a cigarillo, or even so much as a matchstick in hand, you're going straight over the side, got it?"

With a lot of yelling and a flurry of action, the *Dragonfly* was let loose from its moorings. It drifted lazily into the sky, like a child's balloon that had slipped from its sticky, inattentive grasp. On the quarterdeck, Captain Tonbo pulled at a set of levers, adjusting the ship's wings until they caught the breeze, pushing them north towards the city.

From his vantage point up on the forecastle, Dexter was enjoying the sight of John and Agnes getting beasted by the terminally grumpy Jacko. He had them running back and forth, doing things with ropes and barrels that just looked like a lot of busy work to Dexter. Whatever they'd done to get the man's back up so quickly they were probably regretting it right about now.

"Prepare for the push!" yelled the captain as they approached the line of forges along the south side of the river.

"The what?" said John.

"You'll see," said Jacko, going down on one knee.

The airship hit a wall of hot air and shot into the sky. Ropes creaked noisily as the deck tipped steeply upwards, sending John cartwheeling into the wall beneath the captain's feet.

"One hand for yourself and one for the ship, Mr Sinister," said the captain, her eyes on the rigging where it dug into the canvas balloon. John didn't know what she meant so he just clung on like he expected the whole ship to do a loop-de-loop at any moment.

On the forecastle, Dexter had to dig his metal claws in deep as the rush of wind threatened to flip him over the side, gouging ragged grooves into the woodwork as he slid across the deck. Squeezing his eyes shut tight, he tried not to eject a stream of charcoal briquettes out of his back end as his waste management system prepared to flee whatever the hell was going on out there.

As suddenly as it had begun, the wind subsided. The ropes creaked back to their normal lengths, and the deck levelled off to more of a tipsy aunt than a drunken uncle sort of angle.

"What the hell was that?!" said Agnes, letting go of the mast stump she had been clinging on to.

"That were the push," said Jacko with a sly grin. "It's why we ties up at Ship Fields, so's we can get an extra bit o' rise from the forges when we sets off. See?" He pointed over the side at the rapidly diminishing landscape. They were already the highest thing in the sky, and they only kept getting higher.

They could see the whole of Hammersmyth as it fell away beneath them, its grubby greys and smutty blacks a grimy blot on the lush green landscape, like a splat of Gentleman's Relish on a new silk tie. It didn't look half as important or intimidating as it did when you were in among the clash and clatter of its cobblestone streets. Dexter wasn't sure what to think of that. On the one hand it was nice to get a bit of perspective, it gave your life meaning. But on the other hand, to see everything you had ever known all in one place, small and insignificant and rather unimpressive (if you were being honest with yourself) was a tad disconcerting to say the least.

"I can see my house from here!" said Agnes, pointing. "And the club. And there's Jane's house too. Cor!"

"Yeah that's great," said John, turning back towards the deck. He'd gone a funny shade of green.

"Alright, that's enough gawping. Back to work, you two. You! Cabin boy. Belay that line there. And you, get below and make sure nothing's shifted about during take-off."

"And if it has?" said Agnes.

"Fer crying out loud. Then you puts it back where it came from, don'cha? Gordon Bennett, do I 'ave to fink of everyfing meself?"

Deciding he'd had enough of all the shouting for now, Dexter went below, following his nose through the ship's underbelly until it led him to the airship's tiny galley. There he found a large man in a too-small room using a razor-sharp cleaver to chop vegetables.

There was a pot of something delicious bubbling away on the stove and the air had that freshly-baked bread smell that nobody in their right mind could resist. Despite the captain's warning, Dexter was contemplating trying to snaffle some when he heard footsteps coming along the corridor behind him.

Jacko appeared in the doorway of the galley, leaning on the jamb like he was out for his morning stroll. "You met these new recruits then yet?"

"Can't say that I have," said the cook, keeping his attention on his vegetables.

"There's summat not right about 'em," Jacko grumbled.

The cook looked up. "How's that then?"

Jacko shrugged. "Like how neither one of 'em seems daft enough to sign on for a job like this, know what I mean? Makes you wonder if they ain't up to summink."

"Ach, you're being paranoid, boyo," said the cook, going back to his chopping. "I'm sure the captain knows what she's doing."

"Well you just watch what you say around 'em, you hear? We don't need no outsiders interferin' in our business, know what I mean? Don't tell them nuffink about nuffink, got it?"

Abruptly sweeping the chopped vegetables into a bowl, the cook hoiked his cleaver across the room, slamming the blade into the centre of a crudely drawn dart board he had on the wall. "With all due respect, boyo, I ain't the one standing around running my mouth off, am I? Now if you don't mind, I gots cooking to be getting on with."

Turning his back on Jacko, the cook tossed the bowl of vegetables into the pot and gave it a stir.

Jacko pursed his lips, like he had a few choice words he still wanted to say, but instead he slinked off back down the narrow corridor, grumbling all the way.

Slipping out from his hiding place, Dexter went on deck to look for John.

Molly Sigurdsson, leader of the Western Riders, sat stoking the fire as she waited for Fenris Wolf, leader of the Northern Wolves, to arrive.

The large cave that the Western Riders called home was an old slate quarry, a man-made hole in the side of a hill the kind of which you got all over the Lake District. But whereas most of them were small and cramped and thoroughly unpleasant, this one was big enough to fit an airship, with room left over for a small campsite and storage area.

Most of the cave floor was taken up by a deep pool of water that extended beyond the cave mouth, and it was there that the Riders' airship, the *Molly's Kiss*, sat. She floated in the pool like a tiger at rest, tied down so that she didn't puncture her balloon on the jagged roof above.

Molly Sigurdsson hated that her ship was called the *Molly's Kiss*. Named after her mother, as was she, she'd had to endure all kinds of jokes about it growing up, jokes that only ever seemed to be funny to the person saying them. She'd put up with them for as long as she could until one day she could stomach it no longer. She broke a boy's nose, a sneery little brat called Trevor who seemed to take particular pleasure in winding her up. The other kids let her be after that, almost completely in fact, which made for a lonely childhood. She was five years old at the time.

Molly angrily tossed another log on the fire, throwing up a shower of sparks. It wasn't a big fire, and it did little to warm such a vast, open space, but that wasn't why it was there. It was there to provide a light in the darkness, an anchor for little Sue should she need it. Molly glanced over to where Sue was playing by the water's edge, silently building a tower out of small rocks, oblivious to the world. Sue couldn't hear very well, so it helped to have a bit of light so she knew you were coming. Sometimes a shadow moving was all the warning she got that you were there.

Molly caught sight of a figure in the mouth of the cave. "Ho there in the camp! Permission to come in?"

"Come on in, Fenris. And bring Toby in with you an'all."

The two men entered. "I go by Skull these days," said the young lad, sullenly.

"Quiet, boy," said Fenris, positioning himself carefully on a narrow log opposite Molly. "Nobody cares."

"But, Dad—"

"I said enough!"

Toby walked off in a huff (although not so much of a huff that it might make his father mad).

The two leaders considered each other for a moment. "Tea?" said Molly, gesturing to a large pot next to the fire.

Fenris took a good look around the cave like he'd never been there before. "No thanks," he said. "I'd rather drink donkey piss."

"We've nothing stronger I'm afraid. I can offer you some water, if you like?"

Fenris grinned wolfishly. "I'd rather drink tea."

The pleasantries over with, Molly got down to business. "So what can I do for you, Fenris? To what do we owe the honour?"

"Did you hear what happened to the *Dauntless*?"

"Some. I heard your boy got in a fight he wasn't prepared for, her balloon got shot, and she came down somewhere in the woods over the way." Molly gestured vaguely to where the wreck of the *Dauntless* lay smouldering.

"That's about the long and the short of it."

"And now here you are, come to ask if you can borrow the *Kiss*."

Fenris Wolf smiled again. "You never miss a trick, do you, Molly?"

"I find it the best way to stay alive, Fenris."

Fenris nodded. "I hear that." He picked a stick out of the fire and began poking at it. "And you're right, of course. Through a series of unfortunate events, I find myself to be a pirate without a ship, which, I think you will agree, is a rather embarrassing position to be in."

"It happens," said Molly, with a disinterested shrug.

"Indeed it does," said Fenris. "I'm glad you understand." He paused, as if expecting Molly to say more, but she was too busy pouring herself some tea. "So how about it? You reckon you could see your way to lending me the *Kiss* for a wee while?"

"No."

"Now hold on," said Fenris, patting the air. "Hear me out. It'd only be for a few days, just until the Wolves got back on their feet. There's a couple of lucrative jobs coming through, and if we can bag them we'd have enough to get ourselves a new ship. *And* we could even pay you a few bob as, like, rent and that, for you lending us the *Kiss* and everything. It'd be an easy bit of money for you and yours, and you wouldn't have to lift a finger to earn it."

"I understand," said Molly, blowing on her tea.

"So?"

"No."

Fenris stopped playing with the fire. He focussed his attention on Molly. "That's not very friendly of you, Molly."

"Fenris, I'm being as friendly as I can, but if you want the unfriendly version here it is. It's not my fault your boy went and crashed your ship. He's the one with sawdust for brains, not me."

Fenris's expression darkened. "That's not a very nice thing to say."

"Believe me, that's as nice as it gets."

"The Wolves need use of a ship. We can't make money without it."

"Not my problem, pal. It's not my job to keep the Northern Wolves in the air."

The two fell silent as they watched each other, both very aware of where the nearest knives were. Then Fenris Wolf gave an exaggerated shrug. "Well, I'm sorry to hear that," he said, tugging on his ear. "Still, I get where you're coming from. And you can't blame a man for trying, now can you."

"No, you can't," said Molly.

"I would have liked it if we could have come to some kind of arrangement, but I guess things being what they are, that—"

There was a sudden clatter of falling rock. Fenris and Molly looked over to where Sue was sitting by her collapsed tower, her eyes wide. She made a quick series of gestures as she glanced behind Molly, looking worried. Molly smiled and gestured back, which seemed to calm her down some.

"What's going on?" said Fenris. "What's with all the—?" He threw his hands around vaguely in front of him.

"Oh nothing," said Molly, returning to her tea. "She's trying to warn me about your boy Toby sneaking up behind me. But what she and Toby don't know is that behind him is my brother, Magnus, holding a very large, very lethal crossbow."

Fenris looked past Molly, and past his knife-wielding son, to where Magnus Sigurdsson was stepping out of the shadows hold-ing what was indeed a very large, very lethal crossbow. "Morning, fellas. Long time no see."

Fenris's shock and indignation was well rehearsed. "Toby! What the hell do you think you're doing? Why are you sneaking around back there?"

"What? I– No, nuthin'. I was just walking about a bit, that's all."

"With your knife out?" said Magnus.

"No, I didn't. I mean, I were looking at it and that, yeah, but I wasn't doing nuthin'. Honest."

"Come here, boy!"

Toby skulked round to his father's side, catching a clip round the ear for his troubles. "Apologise at once, do you hear!"

"Sorry," Toby mumbled.

Fenris looked grief-stricken. "Molly, I'm so sorry about this misunderstanding. I know how it must look. As you say, my boy really does have sawdust for brains sometimes. I hope you won't hold it against him? I'd hate for something like this to spoil the special relationship between our respective clans."

Molly glanced up at her brother, who seemed about as impressed by that statement as she was. "Take it from me, Fenris. Relations between our two clans remain as cordial as they ever were."

Fenris clasped his hands together in joy. "Wonderful. I'm so glad to hear it. Now, if you'll excuse me, I must be off. Things to do, and all that. I'll see you soon, Molly. Magnus. You two take care now."

"You too," said Molly, watching both men's hands as they headed for the exit. "You too."

Outside, Fenris's donkey stood watching the cave mouth with an air of hereditary suspicion. It had never been below ground before, but like all of the mules that traversed the Lake District's highways and byways it came from a long line of creatures that had known nothing but the endless dragging of carts of ore along dark narrow tunnels with nary a kind word or friendly gesture from the moment they were born until the day they collapsed under the strain of the yolk, their bodies left to rot on the heaps of spoil they had spent their entire lives creating. As such, it expected bad things to come from dark places, so it wasn't surprised when its current burden came storming out of the shadows, fists clenched, and booted a large rock past its not inconsiderable head. It was more surprised that the rock missed than anything else. Getting hit in the head by unexpected rocks summed up your average donkey's philosophy on life in a nutshell.

Climbing astride his donkey, Fenris kicked it to a trot, forcing the animal down the rocky hillside faster than was probably wise, the donkey only too happy to oblige if it meant getting away from that massive menacing maw.

Toby watched his father head downhill in a cloud of dust. Only when it became apparent that he wasn't about to wait for him did he set off after, slipping more than once as he stumbled his way down the rocky slope.

John Sinister sat cross-legged on the deck of the *Dragonfly* trying to untangle a Gordian knot of rope bigger than his head. He suspected from the gleeful way Jacko stood nearby watching him struggle that the bosun had created it on purpose to mess with him, a likely scenario considering how clean and tidy the rest of the ship was. After two hours of organising what was already a very organised ship, Jacko had clearly run out of things for them to do.

"Mr Sinister, a word if you would, please," called the captain from the quarterdeck. "Mr Jackson, would you inform Mr Jones that we will be arriving in Iron Bridge shortly, and that he may serve lunch then."

"Aye, Captain," said Jacko, reluctantly. He went below, watching John every step of the way.

John joined the captain on the quarterdeck. "What can I do for you, Captain?"

"I was wondering how you intend to pursue your investigation? I hope you are not planning on sitting around here waiting for us to get attacked?"

"Er, no indeed," said John, mentally crossing that option off the list. "Um, well, first off, why don't you tell me what you can about these sky pirates? Where they come from, how long they've been around, that kind of thing."

Captain Tonbo thought for a moment. "I cannot tell you much more than Mr Frobisher could. These pirates have always been a menace, but recently they have become much more aggressive and much better informed. I suspect that someone somewhere is passing them information for money."

"Who?"

"If we knew that, Mr Sinister, you would not be here."

"Right. Of course. So, where would you start, if you were me? Who would you want to talk to first?"

The captain considered for a long while. "I would speak to the other captains, see what they have to say on the matter."

"That's going to be a little hard to do from up here."

"Once we have our cargo we will over-night at an inn in the Lake District. There are usually a few captains around. I can arrange a meeting. I cannot guarantee they will answer your questions, but you will get a chance to ask them at least. It might be very revealing, either way."

"Let's hope," said John, earning himself a dubious look from Captain Tonbo.

Appearing back on deck, Jacko was surprised to find John still on the quarterdeck. "You better get back to work before Mr Jackson's suspicions are aroused. If he works out what you are up to the whole world will know by the end of the day."

"Right. But you've got to tell him to lay off a bit. I can't investigate anything if I'm scrubbing decks all day."

The captain nodded. "I will have a word when we come in to land."

John went back to his ropework. He'd made very little headway when Dexter sidled up, the mechanical cat checking the coast was clear before speaking. "Having fun?"

"Yeah. So much fun it should be illegal. Where have you been?"

"Oh, y'know, just looking around."

"Find anything interesting?"

"Not really. Everything's pretty ship shape and Bristol fashion down below, although I did hear quite an interesting conversation between our boy Jacko and the cook."

"Oh yeah? How so?"

"They didn't go into specifics, but there's definitely something going on round here, and whatever it is, everyone was very keen for everybody else to keep their mouths shut about it."

"Really? That's good to know. Nice work, Dexter."

"Hey, I'm not just a pretty face, y'know. So what now?"

"Well, the captain's going to arrange for me to meet with some of the other captains, see what they've got to say for themselves. In the meantime we carry on, keep our heads down, and try not to raise any suspicions. We need to see what we can figure out before anyone knows what we're up to."

Dexter chuckled. "Don't worry about me, my son. You've got to get up pretty early in the morning to catch me doing anything I—"

At the far end of the deck, Dexter caught sight of Agnes watching the pair of them. How long she'd been watching he couldn't say. She was frowning the way someone does when they discover their keys aren't where they left them last night; mildly puzzled, but not overly concerned. Glancing left and right Dexter fake-coughed up a hairball, whispering, "Later," out the side of his mouth, before disappearing back below decks.

Smiling reassuringly at Agnes, John went back to finding out if he was about to become the future king of Asia or knot.

"Standby the ropes! Mr Jackson, the bell, if you please."

Dropping down into Iron Bridge Gorge, the *Dragonfly* drifted north along the river, weaving her way through a forest of tall soot-blackened chimneys and spindly iron winch towers. She headed for a large cobbled courtyard by the river's edge, descending into the cacophony of clangs and clatters that was a sure sign of progress and innovation.

Hanging off the front of the ship, Jacko rang a highly-polished brass bell, causing a flurry of activity in the courtyard below. Young boys ran from all over to form an oval into which the *Dragonfly* quickly sank. Shielding their eyes against the sun, they waited for the ship to come ever closer.

"Away the lines!" yelled the captain.

John and Agnes ran down either side of the ship tossing coils of rope over the edge. As they dropped down on their heads, the boys ran with them to iron loops set into the ground. Looping the ropes through, they heaved as one, bringing the airship in to rest a few feet above the grimy cobbles. Tying off their ropes, the boys disappeared once more, back to whatever duties had been abandoned when the bell rang out.

There was a wooden scaffold next to the airship, a zig-zag of ramps that led up to a wide platform onto which a hand-crank crane had been fitted. Captain Tonbo tossed out a plank to bridge the gap between the platform and the ship.

"I will go see about our cargo. The rest of you see to your bellies. Mr Sinister, you are with me."

John would much rather have seen to his belly as well – he'd had nothing since breakfast – but he knew better than to argue. "Aye, Captain," he said, doing his best not to sound like a character from a second-rate play. Captain Tonbo almost seemed amused.

"A simple yes ma'am would suffice, Mr Sinister. We are not on the high seas."

"Yes, ma'am," John mumbled.

The captain strode confidently across the rickety gangplank, followed by a more hesitant John, with Dexter tagging along for good measure.

All the way down the wooden scaffold, the cat felt like there were eyes on him, like someone was watching him from above, but when he reached the ground and looked up there was nobody to be seen.

Heading across the bustling courtyard, Captain Tonbo led them over to a short, stocky man whose demeanour had the word 'foreman' written all over it. He had a clipboard in one hand, a large stick in the other, and he was orchestrating the chaos of delivery drivers and workmen like he knew every man's job inside out (and don't you forget it, mind!). A starched shirt with the sleeves rolled up, heaven help the man who made him repeat himself, because he simply didn't have time for such nonsense. "Mr Shuttleworth." The man turned round to reveal the most gloriously bushy moustache John had ever seen.

"Ah! Captain Tonbo. Nice to see you again." Mr Shuttleworth shoved the clipboard under his right arm so he could shake the captain's left hand.

"And you, Mr Shuttleworth. You have my cargo for me?"

Mr Shuttleworth's face darkened. "I do not. Those damn glass blowers are late with their delivery." He checked his watch. "They should have been here over two hours ago."

Captain Tonbo sighed loudly. "So what does that mean?"

"It means another three hours at least before your consignment is ready to load, and that's only if their delivery arrives right this very second." The three of them turned towards the iron gates of the courtyard, which remained stubbornly cart free. "I'm sorry about this, but it's out of my hands. I hope you understand."

"Whether I do or I do not makes no difference. It will not get me loaded any faster, will it?"

"Fair enough," said Mr Shuttleworth. "Come up to the office and we can at least get your paperwork sorted out. That way you can be loaded and off as soon as."

John and the captain followed Mr Shuttleworth to a large building on the south side of the courtyard. Entering through the loading bay, the foreman led them through a warren of workbenches, each one occupied by a grim individual wholly intent upon their work. Mr Shuttleworth greeted them all by name as he went past, enquiring after their families or sharing a quick joke and getting a polite nod or a cheeky comeback in return. Who could get away with what depended on the seniority of the man or the complexity of the task at hand. The more skill a man had the cheekier he was allowed to be; up to a point, of course. By the time they'd made it across three floors and up two flights of stairs, he must have said hello to more than two dozen people, give or take the odd pot boy or two.

The man's office was just as John had expected. A desk, a chair, a row of filing cabinets, and a patented Accuracy Timepiece, the most reliable clock money could buy. It was a place for taking care of business quickly and efficiently, and as such it did not encourage visitors to loiter. There was nowhere for them to sit for a start.

Mr Shuttleworth went behind his desk. Despite the available chair, he chose to remain standing. "Here are your dispatch papers along with an invoice for the goods, to be paid cash on delivery. As usual, the money is to be returned here to me within seven days, minus your own fee, of course."

"Thank you, Mr Shuttleworth." The captain glanced at the paperwork. "What are 'phlogiston collectors'?"

"Damned if I know. They send us the plans and we make 'em. I never ask what they're for. Although these things don't seem to do anything, far as I can tell. Just looks like lot of glass and spinney clockwork bits to me."

With a shrug, the captain put away her papers.

Mr Shuttleworth nodded over at John. "So who's this you've got with you? Bert's replacement? Bit old for a cabin boy, ain't he?"

"This is John Sinister. He has been hired by the Air Couriers Guild to look into our pirate problem." The captain turned to John. "Mr Shuttleworth is the most trustworthy man I know. You can speak freely in front of him."

"You flatter me, Captain Tonbo. Now then... Sinister? Sinister? Seems I know that name from somewhere, do I not?"

"Mr Sinister is the man who brought Donald Chard's killers to justice."

"Good God, so he is! My apologies, sir. How could I forget." Mr Shuttleworth went to shake John's hand, his face full of emotion. "We here at Chard Mechanical can't thank you enough for what you've done. It was hard for us, losing our founder like that, but knowing that those wot done him in might swing for it makes it somewhat easier to bear. If you need anything whilst you're here, anything at all, you let me know."

The man had a hell of a grip, made all the more so by the flood of emotion flowing through him. John politely, but firmly, extricated his poor hand. "Chard Mechanical you say. I had no idea. I didn't see any sign outside."

Mr Shuttleworth chuckled. "There's no need for signs when you own everything."

"Everything?"

"Well, almost everything. If it wasn't for Mr Chard most of us wouldn't be here now. God knows what'll happen now that he's gone. Um…" The ever confident Mr Shuttleworth grew hesitant all of a sudden. "Do you mind if I ask you something? Only we keep hearing these rumours. Is it true, about our new owner? That Mr Chard left the company to some…" Looking down, Mr Shuttle-worth spotted Dexter for the first time. "Cat."

Dexter was very tempted to wink up at him.

"What you heard is true, Mr Shuttleworth. Although I can assure you that they are looking for someone with fewer than four legs to make decisions on the cat's behalf." *They being me, and me not having a clue where to start,* thought John.

"Well, let's hope they find someone who knows their arse from their elbow. That lot down there needs a right good sorting out from what I hear."

"I'm sure they will," said John. "I wouldn't worry about it."

"I'll stop worrying when I know my new boss doesn't lick himself to stay clean," said Mr Shuttleworth, watching Dexter out the side of his eye. "I'm a dog person, Mr Sinister. Always have been. I find that once cats get involved you're just asking for trouble."

Huh. Tell me about it, thought John.

Arriving back aboard the *Dragonfly*, they found everyone on deck enjoying a hearty bowl or three of the most delicious smelling vegetable stew.

"Loading time, Cap'n?" asked the bosun.

"No, Mr Jackson. It is not. There has been some delay. We will not be loading until five o'clock at the earliest."

The bosun frowned. "But that means,"—he counted on his fingers—"it'll be eight, nine o'clock afore we reach Striding Edge." He didn't look too happy about that.

"Indeed," said the captain, equally as unimpressed.

"I don't get it," said John. "Why does that matter?"

"Because Striding Edge is smack dab in the middle of pirate territory, that's why," the bosun replied. "It ain't somewhere you wants to be flyin' around at night, y'understand?"

"I do," said John. He didn't.

"He means we might get attacked," said the captain. "Although that could happen either way, no matter what time of day it is."

"Yeah, but at least durin' the day we can see it comin', like," replied Jacko.

"What're we carrying?" asked Mick the mechanic, surprising everyone. John for one didn't realise he was even there.

"Phlogiston collectors."

Jacko's face took on a confused expression that fit very naturally on him. "You what? What the hell're phlogiston collectors when they're at home?"

"Fragile and expensive," the captain replied. "So when they get here we need to be extra careful with them. But, until then, we have time for a bit of shore leave. Be back by five, and God help you if I smell so much as a hint of booze on any one of you."

Outside the mouth of their cavernous hideout, Molly Sigurdsson and her brother Magnus were watching Fenris and his donkey make their way along the shores of the lake below, pursued by his donkey of a son.

"That was pretty damn brazen, even for Fenris," said Magnus. "I can't believe he would try and pull something like that."

Molly snorted. "I can. He's been getting worse and worse ever since Dad left. It was just a matter of time before he turned on us as well." Molly's father, Magnus Sigurdsson senior, had led the Western Riders until six months ago. He had been a firm but fair man, the one all the other leaders turned to for advice, even Fenris Wolf. When he'd retired from the pirate life, going back to his native Iceland with their mother, Molly (the Sigurdsson's had never been very inventive when it came to naming their two children), he'd left a hole that Fenris Wolf had desperately been trying to fill ever since. But whereas Magnus senior had been a likeable man with all the wisdom and cunning of a chess-playing fox, Fenris had all the brains and subtlety of a man banging his head against a door marked 'pull'.

Magnus stretched, cracking his back loudly in the process. "Well, now that he's lost the *Dauntless* maybe things'll calm down a bit. Trade has been right off with him attacking everything in sight. Not to mention that lad who almost died. I mean, if they hadn't've caught him, that'd be it for us. There'd be cops all over the place and we'd be done for. And then what'd we do? How would we make a livin' then?"

"Yes," said Molly, deep in thought. "How indeed?"

John Sinister lounged against the crane atop the loading scaffold, munching on some dried figs, his reward for a job well done from Mr Jones, the cook.

John had spent the last hour being dragged around Blast Hill – the small town above Iron Bridge Gorge – helping Mr Jones shop for 'vittles', a nautical term which seemed to encompass anything and everything you could think to put in your mouth. It hadn't been the worst job in the world. Mr Jones was a rather jovial Welshman who liked a good natter, so long as the subject was food or food related. As such, John now knew more about the various herbs and spices than he ever thought he would, as well as over a dozen different things you could do with a potato. It had been an experience to say the least. He would have preferred to have followed Mr Jackson, to see what he got up to, but it hadn't been up to him. His pretend duties as cabin boy had had to come first.

Dexter had been tasked with following the bosun, Mr Jackson skulking off shortly after lunch. It had seemed wiser than sending Agnes after him, considering how conspicuous she was. She had remained by the ship, keeping an eye on the mechanic who, according to Mr Jones, everyone referred to as Mick the Spanner (although *never* to his face for some reason) and who was in fact married to Captain Tonbo, which surprised the hell out of John (a common reaction, according to Mr Jones).

John had traded places with Agnes when he came back from shopping, so that she could have a look around before they left. He could see how keen she was to see the beating heart of industrial Britain for herself, even though it was just a lot of forges, furnaces, and factories that all looked the same after a while as far as John was concerned. He had seen more than enough of Iron Bridge when he was there last summer looking for work, so he was happy to stay by the ship watching a man so engrossed in his work he seemed to have no idea how much of his crack was on show every time he bent over.

John watched the chaos of the yard below, fully aware that it was, in fact, running like clockwork. Mr Shuttleworth saw to that. Out of his office again, he went hither and thither, issuing orders in the calm, quiet manner of a man who expected people to do what he said. He didn't even get mad when the delivery they'd been waiting for finally showed up. He simply directed them to the loading bay and crossed it off his list (although John suspected he'd be having a word with someone later about all the trouble they had caused).

John spotted Dexter enter the yard alone. Weaving his way between an ever-changing forest of cartwheels and feet, the cat climbed the scaffold to join his partner's vigil.

"You're back early," said John. "Where's Jacko?"

"Dunno," said Dexter. "I lost him. He went in the pub at Blast Hill and he never came out again. I didn't realise there were two doors, did I? Round the corner from each other. I feel like such an idiot."

John shrugged. "Don't worry about it. He'll show up again soon enough." He took another bite of dried fig. "Did he get up to anything before he gave you the slip?"

"Nothing much. Bought himself a bunch of grapes, two packs of lard, and some comic books. That's about it."

"Comic books? Really?"

"Yeah. You wouldn't think he'd be the type, would you? Still, you never can tell."

"I guess you can't," said John.

They sat for a while watching Mr Shuttleworth taking care of business.

"Listen, I've been thinking," said John.

"Oh well done," said Dexter.

"Y'know how we need someone to take charge of the Transatlantic Air Line, whip it into shape? Well what about our Mr Shuttleworth there? He certainly seem to know his arse from his elbow."

"He does, I'll give you that. But do you think he'd go for it?"

"No idea. But we could ask and find out." They watched Mr Shuttleworth head back inside.

"Sure, why not," said Dexter, pushing himself to his feet. "What've we got to lose."

John and Dexter entered Mr Shuttleworth's office to find the man bent over his desk, studying some paperwork. It looked like that chair of his never got any use.

"Ah! Mr Sinister. I was wondering when you'd come to see me."

"You were?"

"Yes. I imagine you have questions for me regarding this whole sky pirate business."

"Oh right, yes. The sky pirates. Of course. Yes, indeed I do. Many questions, in fact." John quickly came up with some. "Well, to begin with, why don't you tell me what *you* think is going on?"

"About how they know so much, you mean?"

"Yes, that's it. Exactly."

Mr Shuttleworth gave it some thought. "I reckon they've got somebody on the inside. Someone who tells them where to be, who to hit."

"An informant, you mean?"

"That's right. Has to be. No way they could know all the stuff they know without someone telling them first, know what I mean?"

"But who though? Someone on one of the ships?" *Jacko, for instance?*

Mr Shuttleworth shook his head. "I doubt it. Too many people getting hit too many places for that. I reckon you're looking at somebody on the ground. In the guild, maybe. Although more likely you're looking for someone a bit further down the line."

"Like where, for instance?"

"Captain Tonbo said you were headed up to Striding Edge. That'd be a good place to start. There's a lot of trade goes through there. Lots of ships. Lots of information. If there's no one there knows what's going on I'll eat my hat."

"I see. Thank you. That's very interesting."

"My pleasure, Mr Sinister," said Mr Shuttleworth, checking his watch as he glanced out of the window. "Glad to be of assistance." Opening the window he leaned out. "Pete! What are you still doing here? You should have left three minutes ago." John didn't catch Pete's reply. "I don't care what he said, *I'm* telling you to get going. Or do I need to come down there?" There was a crack of a whip and the sound of a cart as it rattled its way across the uneven cobbles. Mr Shuttleworth ducked his head back inside. "Well now, if there's nothing else, Mr Sinister, I've work to be getting on with."

John glanced down at Dexter who gave him a quick nod. "Actually, Mr Shuttleworth, there is one more thing. You remember earlier we were talking about Mr Chard's cat, the one that's inherited his entire company? Well this is him, Mr Chard's cat. His name's Dexter."

"You don't say," said Mr Shuttleworth, regarding Dexter with a mix of admiration, jealousy, and contempt.

"Indeed I do," said John. "Only there's more to it than that. You see, through a bizarre set of circumstances, I have become Dexter's, er, legal representative, of sorts, which means I am, for the moment, in charge of Chard Mechanical... in a way."

"Is that right," said Mr Shuttleworth, shifting his complicated gaze from Dexter to John.

"It is. Although believe me, I wish it wasn't. Which is why I'm looking for someone to take over as general manager as soon as possible, before I go making a right hash of everything."

"That would be the smart thing to do," said Mr Shuttleworth carefully. "Who'd you have in mind?"

"You, Mr Shuttleworth. We'd like to put you in charge of... well, everything."

Mr Shuttleworth sat down slowly. "Please, call me Arthur."

"So what do you say, Arthur? Does it sound like something you'd be interested in?"

Dexter jumped up on the desk and sat down. Arthur Shuttleworth considered the cat for a very long time.

"We could double your salary," said John.

"You'd have to, to pry the missus away from this place."

"Triple then. Or quadruple, even." John had no idea if that was possible, but if the man could get Chard mechanical back in the black he was sure none of the board members would complain.

Arthur looked out the window at the thriving hub of industry and invention that was his entire life. "Do you know what we do here, Mr Sinister?" he said. "We change the world. Day in, day out, we create things that make the world a better place. There's more ingenuity along this riverbank, more creativity and innovation, than you can shake a stick at. We are at the cutting edge of every new technology you can think of, and you want me to go down south and push papers round all day. No, I'm sorry, Mr Sinister, but that does not sound like me. That's some other man's job. I'd rather stay here where the action is. Because I doubt there's owt going on down there that could interest me half as much as what I can see out my window at this very moment."

Dexter chuckled. He looked at John, who gave him an up-to-you kind of a shrug. The cat turned back to Mr Shuttleworth.

"Oh yeah?" said Dexter. "Wanna bet?"

Some of the words Mr Shuttleworth came out with as he fell off his chair John had never heard before, but he understood their meaning well enough.

Chapter 3

Onward To Striding Edge

John Sinister leant against the railing of the airship, looking back at Iron Bridge Gorge as it fell into the distance. It was late. The sun had dropped so low that most of its light was gone from the valley, replaced by the fiery orange glow from all the blast furnaces, foundries, and forges along the river's edge. It was as if a volcano had erupted, filling the river with molten lava, the ripples of heat rising into the air making it seem like the whole valley was on fire.

It was like that every night, John knew, even on Sundays, it being cheaper to keep the forges lit than it was to let them go cold. He couldn't imagine what it was like to live there. The constant noise would drive you up the wall. But at the same time he could see why Mr Shuttleworth had been so reluctant to leave. There was something about the place, about the steady hum of activity, that made you want to roll up your sleeves and get involved.

"How do you think he'll get on?" asked Dexter, from down by John's feet.

"I think he'll be fine. He said he remembers Nomko from the Air Line launch party, so he'll have one friend when he gets there at least." Nomko was the rather young, incredibly clever, slightly eccentric man from Japan who was the Head Engineer at Chard

Mechanical. He was the one responsible for bringing Dexter into the world, an achievement he had been unable to replicate since, no matter how hard he tried.

"I meant with his wife. How do you think he'll get on with her?"

John chuckled. "That I couldn't tell you, but rather him than me. I'm sure she'll be fine with it. Eventually."

Agnes appeared at the railing next to John. Leaning over the side, she checked out the view. "Ain't that something. Almost looks alive, dunnit."

"It does that," said John. "Did you get a good look around while we were there?"

"I did. Thanks for that. I always wondered what they got up to up this way, and now I know." Agnes produced a tissue-wrapped package from her breast pocket. "It's not all heavy industry, y'know. There's a lot of arts and crafts going on as well. I got this for Jane. I thought she might like it." It was a delicate silver necklace with a beautiful little locket hanging from it, the kind in which you kept keepsakes from your loved ones so they would always be near your heart. It struck John as quite an intimate gift to give to a friend.

"She'll love it," he said, which made Agnes smile. She folded the locket back in its tissue paper and put it away carefully. "Say, Agnes, I don't suppose you saw Jacko whilst you were out and about did you?"

"I didn't, no. Why?"

"I was wondering what he got up to, that's all. Trying to figure out if he's part of this whole pirate thing or not." The bosun had arrived back late to the airship, with none of the stuff Dexter had seen him buying, begging the question, what had he done with it all?

"Do you think that's likely?"

"I think it's a possibility."

"Good. I've been looking for an excuse to knock him out ever since we left Hammersmyth."

"Well try and hold off on that for a bit longer. At least until after Striding Edge."

"Why, what's at Striding Edge?"

"Hopefully some answers. From what I hear there's more going on up there than warm beer and a bunk for the night. Think you can keep an eye on him for me, see what he gets up to? I'm going to be busy talking to the other ship captains."

"It would be my pleasure," said Agnes.

Jacko appeared on the deck behind them. "Oi! You two! Quit lolly-gaggin' and get back to work."

"There's nothing to do," said John.

"There's *always* something to do, Cabin Boy," sneered Jacko. "The cook needs a hand in the galley, and I've got a dozen sacks of fruit and veg with your name on it, young lady, so get to it!"

"Fruit and veg? Be we just shifted all that when we set off," said Agnes.

Jacko grinned. "Well now we gotta shift 'em again, don't we. Unless you don't want to muss up them fancy-shmancy pants of yours, that is?"

Agnes looked at John who shook his head gently. "Not yet," he said. "But I promise, if we haven't found anything by this time tomorrow..."

"I'll hold you to that," said Agnes, following Jacko below decks.

"I wouldn't like to be in his shoes this time tomorrow," said Dexter. "Agnes is gonna kill 'im."

John saw no reason to disagree, or to interfere with Agnes when she did.

John entered the galley to find Jones the cook inspecting a bag of potatoes. "Jacko said you needed help?"

Jones squinted over at John. "Does that cat of yours like spuds?" In the corridor, Dexter stopped dead in his tracks.

"I don't think so. Why?"

"Because somebody's been at my Maris Pipers, that's why."

John glanced back at Dexter who did his best to look as if butter wouldn't melt in his mouth. "I'm sure it wasn't him. He knows better than to go stealing other people's food," he said pointedly. Dexter gave him a wink, before swiftly retreating back down the corridor.

Jones picked up a very sharp knife. "You better be right, boyo, for his sake," he said. "If I finds him with his snout in my vittles..." He waved the knife about in an unfriendly manner. "Anyway, we needs to be cracking on, like. There's supper to be made, and all this needs squaring away toot sweet. Think you can find a home for it all?" Jones gestured vaguely at the array of shelves and cupboard around the room. Every available space had been turned into some kind of storage, and they were all pretty full already.

"I'll give it a try," said John.

"Lovely," said Jones, clearing some room so he could start to cook.

There was a large chopping board attached by a couple of thick leather straps to what remained of the ship's mast, which ran up through the centre of the room. Unbuckling it, Jones squeezed it onto the narrow workbench, where he set about chopping the potatoes into tiny, bite-sized pieces. "Leave me out the leeks. I'll be needing those."

John put the leeks to one side. "So, Mr Jones, how long have you been aboard the *Dragonfly*?"

"Oh, I've been with her since the very beginning, I have. Going on a year or so now."

"A year? That's funny. For some reason I thought she'd been flying for longer than that."

"Nope. Mick and the captain put to the skies not long after the trade wars ended." Although everyone referred to the Empire's attempts to open up trade with Japan as the 'Japanese trade wars' they were officially known as The Britannic Oriental Free Trade Negotiations, because there was yet to be a government who wouldn't try to put a shine on a steaming pile of foreign policy by giving it a fancy sounding name. "That's where the two of them met, see, in the Land of the Rising Sun. They came back, got married, and set up the Dragonfly Delivery Company." Jones stopped his chopping to lean in towards John. "Between you and me, I don't think her da approved of the match all that much."

"I see. Well that explains the uniform I suppose, although I still don't get how they ended up together. How does a guy like Mick get someone like Captain Tonbo?"

"I think you're getting the cart before the horse there, boyo. It'd be Captain Tonbo who got a fella like Mick. I know it's hard to tell to look at him, but Mick's got it where it counts." Jones tapped the side of his head with his very sharp knife. "He built the captain's arm from scratch, and he's the one worked out how to make the *Dragonfly* fly like she does. When it comes to them there mechanicalisms our Mick's as sharp as they come. To a woman who values such things he's quite the catch."

"You don't say," said John. "Goes to show, you never can tell, can you. And what about you, Mr Jones? Is there a Mrs Jones somewhere, awaiting her chance to criticise your cooking?"

"Sadly, no. I've not had time for all that malarkey. My work here keeps me fairly busy, and before this I was head cook at the Buddhi temple over in Colwyn Bay, so my chances of meeting a future Mrs Jones have been slim to none for a while now, more's the pity."

"The Buddhi temple? So you were a monk, were you?"

Jones laughed. "Lord, no. I haven't the devotion for that. But I read the books and followed the code, lived it as best I could. It was enough for me."

"And do you follow it still? The Buddhi code, I mean?" *Whatever that is.*

"I do, more or less. It's not so easy once you're out of the temple, but I does what I can."

John looked down at the many boxes of grains, pulses, and lentils, yet to be put away. "That explains the lack of meat, I guess," he said, checking under a bag of onions for any unexpected pork chops.

"Aye. You'll be getting good food whilst you're on board, but not if it once had a face. I may not be a monk, but that's one part of the Buddhi code I'll always stick to no matter what."

John glanced over towards the door where a leather butcher's apron and a brutally large meat tenderiser hung side-by-side on a couple of nails.

"That were me da's," said Mr Jones, following his gaze. "And his da's before that. And his da's before that. I comes from a long line of butchers, me. The Joneses have been chopping meat since Owain Glyndŵr told the English to go stick it where the sun don't shine."

"So what did your dad say when you gave up eating meat?"

"Not a lot," said Mr Jones. "He's dead."

Jones went back to chopping his potatoes, whilst John just stood there trying to figure out if he should apologise or not.

John and Agnes lay in the crews quarters, finally getting a bit of ship-board rest. Whatever the captain had said to Jacko seemed to have done the trick. He hadn't been after them with some menial task that had to be done right away for over an hour now.

John was squeezed onto a narrow bunk barely as wide as a man's forearm, on a horse-hair mattress that was almost as hard as the wood beneath. Agnes was in a hammock strung from one corner of the room to the other, swinging gently with the rocking of the ship. It didn't look very comfortable to John, being all wrapped up like a kipper like that, but Agnes couldn't have been happier. According to her it was snug as anything, and she liked how it reminded her of life on the high seas.

"Did you know that the phrase 'show a leg' comes from the Royal Navy? Sailors used to have to stick a leg out of a morning to show they were awake and ready for action." Agnes swung a leg over the side of the hammock to demonstrate.

"Is that right," said John, shuffling for the umpteenth time as he tried in vain to get comfortable.

"Yup. Those that didn't, ran the risk of getting tumbled out of bed."

"Don't tell Jacko that. You don't want to give him any ideas."

Agnes swung her leg back inside. "Hah. I'd like to see him try."

Jacko appeared in the doorway of the crews quarters looking worried. "On deck, you two, and quick about it. We're coming up on the Lake District."

John pushed himself upright. "Why? What's—?" he started to ask, but Jacko was already gone.

The deck of the *Dragonfly* was cold and dark. All the lamps had been shuttered, and the only sound was the whisper of the wind and the distant creak of rigging high above their heads. John and Agnes emerged on deck to find Jacko waiting for them.

"You two, up the back with the captain. And go softly now. Either of you makes any noise you'll have me to answer to, understand?"

John looked around. Mick was on the forecastle, staring out into the darkness, with Mr Jones keeping watch along one side, whilst Jacko went to stand guard along the other. Heading up onto the quarterdeck, John and Agnes approached the captain at the wheel.

"We are about to enter pirate territory," she said softly. "Everyone needs to keep watch until we reach Striding Edge. Mr Sinister, I want you on the port side. Miss Dexter, the starboard. You see anything you are unsure about you let me know. But do it quietly. Sounds travels a long way up here."

Looking towards the front of the ship, John quickly ran through in his head – *Post script; P.S.; Port, Starboard* – and went to the left-hand side, whilst Agnes went to the right. He looked out over the dark, mountainous landscape, a jagged line the border between the black below and the blue-tinged sky above. There were dots of light amongst the black – farmhouses maybe, or tiny villages – but they were few enough and far between. Mostly the Lake District was all mountains, and lakes, and fields, and fells.

And sheep, John knew. Lots and lots of sheep.

John looked ahead to where the moonlight reflected off a long sweep of water, one of the lakes that gave the area its name. The captain appeared to be steering a path to fly its full length, what

John estimated to be a good ten to fifteen miles or so (although that was a city boy's guess, at night, from the air, with no frame of reference, so it was probably wrong).

Something caught John's eye. There was a light. And movement. Torches on the hillside. Close, but not so close that you could spit on them, even if you put your back into it. John waved to Captain Tonbo, who in turn waved for Agnes to join her at the helm.

"Hold her steady, Miss Dexter," she said, putting Agnes behind the wheel. "Straight on down the lake." Stepping over to John, the captain looked to where he was pointing. "Ah. Well spotted, Mr Sinister."

"What is it? Is it the sky pirates?"

"In a way. They were the sky pirates before the sky pirates got their hands on their own airships. What you have there is a manned harpoon gun, built on one of the highest hills they have this side of Lake Windermere. There are a few of them about. It is how they used to get us before we got wise to what they were up to. Now we avoid them by staying over low land, away from the hilltops, and flying up the lakes whenever we can. Do not worry, they cannot reach us at this distance."

John watched as the torches retreated into their little hut, no doubt to wait for a more hapless, less experienced captain to come their way.

They flew the length of the lake without incident, silvery moonlight reflecting off its choppy waters, then crossed some low ground to sail along another lake, the hills either side of them growing ever higher. Another patch of land, another lake, then they headed up a long valley, the captain pitching the ship nose up to keep them above the slowly rising earth below.

"Keep an eye out behind, you two," said the captain, her own eyes fixed firmly on the horizon up ahead. "If they come now, that is where they will be coming from." John and Agnes both turned to look behind them, but all they could see was the receding lake and a multitude of stars, the likes of which you didn't get in the big city.

The *Dragonfly* reached the top of the valley, where the land levelled off. Captain Tonbo glanced up to her right. "Hang on to something." Yanking one of the levers next to her, she spun the wheel, sending the ship rocketing up the hillside.

Sheep scattered as the *Dragonfly's* hull skimmed over their heads, bleating their disdain as they ran for cover. John and Agnes clung on for dear life as the ship's nose tipped ever higher, the rest of the crew merely shifting their weight to accommodate the deck's increasing lean. The ship could have been at rest for all they seemed to care.

The land rushed by below until, like a breaching whale, the *Dragonfly* burst into the air, leaping from the mountain top into the open skies above.

The captain reset the levers, adjusting the ship's wings back to normal. Correcting her course, she pointed to their destination up ahead. "Striding Edge."

At the summit of Helvellyn, over three-thousand metres above sea level, stood The Inn at the Striding Edge. An ominous grey pile with thick slate walls and small, mean windows, its two storeys were topped by a solidly-built thatched roof, whose hay-bale yellow had succumbed to the immovable greyness of the mountain long ago. Someone had tried to paint the inn white once, to make it seem more inviting, but the wind and rain had stripped the stone bare, leaving jagged white trails along the mortar, a thin veneer of respectability on what was otherwise a fairly disreputable facade.

It had two flaming braziers out front, on long metal poles, to light the way for the terminally lost and the determined to be drunk. Their flickering light cast such stark shadows on the inn it was like watching a charcoal sketch by the most morose of artists being made and re-made over and over again.

"We will be alright from here on," said Captain Tonbo. "Even the sky pirates respect the sanctity of the inn."

"What sanctity?" asked John.

"The inn's a port," said Agnes. "No one messes around in port. If you do, you don't get taken care of. You don't get no water, you don't get no vittles, you don't get nuthin'."

"Quite right, Miss Dexter. Striding Edge is the only place for miles where you can top up the gas you need to make your ship fly." The captain pointed to a geyser of pipework that sprung out of the ground at the far end of the mountain plateau. "Anyone causing trouble round here would soon wish they had not, so mind your manners as you make your enquiries. I should not like to find myself friendless in the Lake District. It would be the death of the *Dragonfly*."

"Don't worry," said John. "Agnes and I are the very souls of discretion. We can make enquiries without it seeming like we're making enquires at all. The locals won't even know they're being enquired up. Will they, Agnes?"

"Er, yeah. Sure. Whatever you say, boss."

"That is wonderful," said the captain. "But a simple please and thank you now and then will probably do the trick."

The captain adjusted the sails to bring the ship around the inn, dropping her lower as they came in to land. "Ready the hook, Mr Jackson," she called, as she steered the ship towards a massive iron loop embedded in the ground.

With Mick hanging on to the back of his belt in case he went over, Jacko dangled a grappling hook over the side of the ship. Hooking it into the iron loop with a quick flick of the wrist, he wrapped the rope round a mechanical winch, he and Mick reeling the ship in by hand as the *Dragonfly* came to a surprisingly smooth, if somewhat sudden, stop.

There were two other airships tied up next to the inn, an old ship of the line gone to seed – a fat bulldog that still remembered its glory days even if no one else did – and a converted tramp steamer with huge scooping sails where its two paddle wheels once stood, suspended from two long narrow balloons that were pointed at both ends. "Ah, good," said Captain Tonbo. "The *Titan* and the *Split* are in. Looks like you will get your conference after all, Mr Sinister."

Whilst Jacko and Mick went to secure the ship, Captain Tonbo took Agnes to check on the cargo, passing Dexter on the stairs as they went below. The cat, all wide eyed and dishevelled, staggered over to John looking like he'd just had a fight with a mangle and lost.

"What happened to you?" said John.

Dexter gave John a hunted look. "You tell me! There I was, mindin' my own business, having a nap on a bag of carrots, when the next thing I know the whole world turns upside down and the bag of carrots is on top of me!"

John laughed. "Yeah, I guess we did come in a little quick, didn't we. You okay? Nothing broken at all?"

"A few carrots and my sense of direction," said Dexter, wandering over to the side of the ship. "So this is Striding Edge, is it? What a dump."

"I've seen worse."

"Yes, I bet you have."

"Listen, do me a favour, when we get in there have a look around, see if you can see anything nefarious going on. From what I hear there's bound to be something."

"No problem. And if I do see something?"

"Let me know and we'll figure it out from there. Don't go giving yourself away. We need to keep a low profile for now, got it?"

Dexter smiled sweetly. "But of course. Absolutely. A low profile. Wouldn't dream of doing anything else."

Despite its remote location, the saloon bar of The Inn at the Striding Edge was as busy as any John had ever seen. The crews of the *Titan* and the *Split* were there of course, taking up either end of the massively long table which ran down the centre of the room, their two captains occupying one of several smaller tables over by the fireplace. And there were a bunch of sheep farmers in, recognisable by their flat caps, walking sticks, and incomprehensible accents – "Didst tha see l'al Jack get chessed by one'a Auld Tom's yows las' Sun'ay week? 'E shot awer yon five-bar yat like the Devil hi'sel were up 'im!" – enjoying a good natter whilst in front of the fire the ram of one and the border collie of another seemed to have come to an uneasy alliance, each pretending the other didn't exist as they lay side by side, warming themselves by the fire's smouldering coals.

The crew of the *Dragonfly* – all except for Mick who, like a proper engineer, had chosen to stay on board to tinker about with something – made their way to the bar. There they were greeted by a warm and ready smile on one of the toughest looking men John had ever seen.

Mr Jones had told John a story about the innkeeper at the Striding Edge, how he'd carried the inn's huge oak table all the way up the mountain by himself, lugging the giant lump of wood on his back like it was made of nothing but fresh air and fairy dust, and whilst John had remained sceptical about the idea, especially after seeing the size of the table involved, he could well believe it now that he'd met the innkeeper himself. The man was massive.

"Good t'see you again, Captain Tonbo," said the giant behind the bar, delicately polishing glasses as if he wasn't big enough to crush rocks with his bare hands. "What can I get you?"

"A warm port for me, if you would, Michael, plus whatever everyone else is having." Leaving the innkeeper to sort out the drinks, Captain Tonbo went over to talk to the two captains.

As he ordered his drink, Mr Jones placed a polished wooden box onto the bar. Leaning on it with his elbow, he gestured to one of the men at the big table, shrugging as if to say, "Well?" The man smiled, drawing his finger across his throat, and the two men laughed.

"Tidy," said Mr Jones, retrieving his drink. "If you folk'll excuse me, I've a game to be getting on with."

"A game?" said John. "What kind of game?"

"Oh, just a little Five Spice Poker between me and the boys. Nothing to write home about."

"Poker? I like a bit of poker. Any chance I can join a bit later, maybe?"

"In theory, Mr Sinister, that'd be fine, but I'm guessing you don't have anything on you to bet with, which is a bit of a problem, see?"

John was indignant. "I have cash, y'know. I'm not poor or anything."

Mr Jones winked. "As I said, boyo, this is Five Spice Poker." He patted his wooden box lovingly. "We don't play for cash." He wandered off to join two other men, both with boxes of their own, at one of the small tables.

Jacko didn't bother making his excuses. He got his drink and headed straight for another of the small tables, some more of the big table peeling off to join him. As far as John could tell they all had something of the bosun about them; mean, miserable, and looking for someone to take it out on. It seemed that whenever a number of ships got together the various ranks would seek each other out, finding comfort in having someone of equal standing to moan about all those above and below them to.

Without a word, Agnes took her drink and went to sit a couple of tables away from the three bosuns, her back to them but her ear very much turned in their general direction. Dexter likewise slinked off towards the other end of the room, slipping beneath the large table before anyone could notice he was there.

"Well now," said the innkeeper, bringing John his drink. "You two must be the new crew of the *Dragonfly*, yes?"

"That's right. I'm the new cabin boy, and Agnes is… whatever the captain needs her to be, I guess."

"The new cabin boy? You're a bit old for a cabin boy, aren't you?"

John shrugged. "What can I say? I need the money."

The innkeeper nodded sagely. "I hear that. Times is tough all round."

"Aren't they always."

"Indeed," said the innkeeper, walking off to attend to another customer.

Looking along the bar, John spotted a young man in a mis-matched set of ill-fitting tweeds playing cards with a seri-ous-faced young girl. They seemed to be playing Happy Families, using a series of hand gestures to indicate which card they were after. The young man was making a big show of how much fun he was having, in a way that was all too familiar to John (he'd done the same thing many times over the years trying to entertain his niece, Emily) and whilst the little girl seemed to be having fun too, she also seemed to be determined to win, judging by the look of concentration on her face.

Captain Tonbo joined John at the bar. "The captains have agreed to speak with you." She waved the innkeeper over. "Michael, may we use your back room. There is something the other captains and I need to discuss in private."

"Of course, Captain. Please, be my guest."

"Thank you." Captain Tonbo led John down a passageway beside the bar, the other two captains joining them after what they considered a discreet pause (which of course was noticed by all, even the sheep).

There were two rooms at the back of the inn. One was the ladies' lounge, which never got any use and so was always full of empty beer barrels and Christmas decorations. The other was a small dining room which likewise got very little use, but which was at least kept clean and tidy should anyone have the sudden urge to celebrate something they didn't fancy celebrating in the main bar; which thus far had yet to happen.

The three captains and John gathered in the dining room, sitting around its mostly round table like four points on a very wonky compass. John found himself with Captain Tonbo on one side and a fat bearded man, who had a penchant for war medals and liquorice cheroots, on the other, whilst across the table a handsome woman several years his senior kept smiling at him between hefty swigs of some foul-smelling wine like she wanted to teach him a thing or two about life (whether he had any interest in learning about such things or not).

"Thank you both for coming," said Captain Tonbo. "As I mentioned earlier, this is John Sinister, the man who discovered Donald Chard's killer. He has been hired by the guild to look into our pirate problem. Mr Sinister, may I present to you Captain Edward Pike of the *Titan*, and Captain Amelia Grant of the *Lickety Split*."

"So you're the famous Mr Sinister," said Captain Grant with a sly grin. "We've heard a lot about you, haven't we, Captain Pike?" The other captain harrumphed his agreement. "They say you're one of the smartest men in the Britannic Empire. Is that true?"

"I wouldn't believe everything you read in the papers," said John, blushing under the captain's intense gaze.

"Pity," said the captain, tossing John a cheeky wink.

"So what makes you think you can sort these pirates out then?" barked Captain Pike.

"Because I may not be one of the smartest men in the empire," said John, "but I can still give them a run for their money if necessary."

"Yes, I'll bet you can," said Captain Grant.

"So you think you're better than us, do you?" Captain Pike growled. "That we're just a bunch of dumb ships' captains who can't take care of themselves, is that it?"

"Oh for heaven's sake," said Captain Grant. "That's not what he's saying at all, are you, Mr Sinister?"

"No, of course not."

"But he is though, isn't he! I can see it in his eyes. He thinks we're a bunch of dullards, too thick to take on a load of pirates by ourselves. Go on, admit it. That's what you think, isn't it!"

"Captain Pike, Mr Sinister is here to help," said Captain Tonbo

"Hah! Sure he is." Grabbing a bottle of wine, Captain Pike sulked down into his chair.

"Ignore him, John," said Captain Grant, leaning forward. "Why don't you go ahead and ask your questions. You have my undivided attention." John felt something rub up against his leg. He looked at Captain Grant, who gave him a coy, lop-sided little smile. "Well?"

"Err, um, urp—" said John.

"Two dill."

"One ginger."

"I'll see your ginger, and raise you some coriander."

Mr Jones considered his cards carefully. "Call," he said, tossing a couple of packets from his little wooden box into the pot.

From his perch up on the shelf, Dexter shook his head. *Bad move, Jonesy*, he thought. *You're gonna regret that.*

Having very quickly gotten bored of listening to drunk people insult each other, Dexter had decided to go find out what Five Spice Poker was all about. From what he could see it appeared to be the same as regular poker except instead of cash the players gambled with a vast array of herbs and spices. That was what the little wooden boxes were about. They each contained dozens of folded up paper packets annotated with the name and weight of their contents, the relative value of which the players seemed to understand instinctively. Dexter had no idea why four basil was worth two cinnamon, which in turn was worth one turmeric, they just were.

As well as the cooks from the other two ships, Mr Jones had been joined by the cook from The Inn at the Striding Edge, a certain Mrs Mulligan. A jolly woman with frizzy blonde hair, she looked like she should be married to Santa Claus, but she played cards with the ruthless efficiency of an executioner who got paid by the slice. She had won the first two hands with ease, and as far as Dexter could tell she was well on her way to winning the third. Of the three hands he could see from his perch up on the shelf, hers was the best, and, looking at the cards on the table, he doubted Mr Jones had anything in his hand that could beat it.

Everyone at the table matched Jones's bet and they laid down their cards.

Mrs Mulligan won, and as she gathered up her winnings with the kind of smile it was hard to stay mad at, Dexter chuckled to himself, nodding as if to say, *See! I told you so.* Then he noticed Mr Jones watching him, a slightly puzzled look upon his face.

Dexter winked at the cook who, to his credit, only let his mouth fall open a little, and he didn't drop any of his cards.

Like Dexter, Agnes too was starting to get bored. The conversation between the three bosuns was as entertaining as you would expect a conversation between three Jackos to be. They sat there nursing their pints as they put the world to rights, every asinine statement greeted by a series of grunted agreements. To hear them tell it they were the only smart, honest, hard-working people in the world, and everybody else was either dumb, lazy, or too dumb to realise how lazy they actually were.

The door of the inn swung open and someone entered. A flash of silence shot around the room. Agnes turned slowly to see who it was.

A tall, slim, good looking black man stood in the doorway of the inn, sporting a very neat and entirely fetching policeman's uniform. He stood surveying the inn's patrons like he knew what they'd been up to but was willing to let it go, for now. Only when his gaze came to Agnes did it pause for any length of time.

"Ah! Constable Kent. How wonderful to see you again," called Michael the innkeeper. "What can I get you? On the house, of course."

The policeman went over to the bar, and as the room slowly returned to normal, Agnes went back to her fruitless eavesdropping.

Against her better judgement, she glanced over her shoulder. The policeman had paid for his drink and was heading in her direction. She looked away, trying to be invisible. *Damn,* she thought. *Why me? Why is it always me?*

"May I join you?" said a deep, confident voice.

"Be my guest," said Agnes, being sure to smile in the way she had learned you should when dealing with the police.

The policeman made a slight bow of thanks and he sat. "I haven't seen you in here before. Are you crew?"

"I am. With the *Dragonfly*." Short and sweet. That was the way to answer the police, with enough information to keep them happy, but no more than was strictly necessary.

"The *Dragonfly*? Captain Tonbo's ship. That's a good crew to be on. I hear she knows her stuff."

"Well she hasn't done anything stupid yet, far as I can tell."

The policeman laughed. "John Kent," he said, offering Agnes his hand.

"Agnes Dexter," said Agnes, only just remembering her current pseudonym in time.

"A pleasure to meet you, Miss Dexter. So tell me, have you been flying long?"

"First day actually. I was brought on board as extra security should they run into trouble."

"Ah yes, the incident with the cabin boy. That was unfortunate."

Suddenly Agnes was all ears. Whilst she knew something had happened to the previous cabin boy she had yet to find a way to broach it naturally with any of the crew. "Were you involved with what happened with…?"

"With Bert? No, not at all. I mean, yes, you could say it was within my jurisdiction, the attack being not too far from here, but seeing as how it happened several hundred feet in the air, and I have yet to learn how to fly, there wasn't much that I could do about any of it." The policeman took a sip of his drink. "Besides, they caught the lad before he fell to his death, and from what I hear the ship that attacked them is now no more, so I'd say it all worked out in the end."

"Why? What happened to the ship that attacked them?"

John Kent considered Agnes for a long while. "You do not seem like your usual deckhand, Miss Dexter. You seem…"—the policeman lowered his voice slightly—"smarter than most."

Agnes smiled, a genuine smile this time. "And you do not seem like your usual policeman, Mr Kent. You're willing to answer questions as well as ask them, for one thing."

"That's probably because you're used to dealing with the police in the big city," said Constable Kent. "London, judging by your cock-a-knee accent."

"Hammersmyth, these days."

"Either way, we do things a bit different up here. You have to, when there's one policeman per hundred square miles or so. I find you get more done with a smile and a quiet word than you ever would treating everyone like a potential criminal, even if most of them are up to something they shouldn't be." He dropped his voice low again. " Or, should I say, especially so." The policeman chuckled, and Agnes couldn't help but join in.

"So tell me, Constable Kent, are you local? Or did they draft you in from elsewhere to keep the peace."

"Oh, I'm local alright. My father came over from the West Indies with his former boss, married my mother, a local woman, and they had half a dozen kids between them, including me. And what about yourself? Are you a Londoner born and raised?"

"Raised, yes. Born, no. My parents came over from Nigeria when I was two."

"And how was it growing up in the capital's east end? A bit different to village life I'll bet."

"Like I said, I moved to Hammersmyth soon as I could."

John Kent nodded. He took another sip of his drink. "So are you married, Miss Dexter?"

Agnes might have choked on her drink if she hadn't seen it coming a mile away. "You don't mess around, do you, Constable Kent?"

The constable laughed. "I do not, Miss Dexter, no. Much better to be direct than mess around being all coy and that I reckon. Life'd be a helluva lot simpler if we were all just open and honest with each other, don't you think?"

Agnes gave a non-committal shrug. Direct was one thing, she'd always been a fan of direct, but open and honest was something else entirely.

"Well with that in mind," she said. "Maybe you can help me out with something?"

Dexter stared at Jones the cook, willing him to look up. The man was about to fold, he could tell, and he didn't have to. The cook from the *Titan* was bluffing. He'd made a big bet, hoping to bully his way into winning the pot, but he had nothing to back it up with.

So long as Jones had a half-way decent hand he'd beat the man hands down. He just needed to go for it!

But he was going to fold. Dexter could see he was going to fold. He kept staring at his opponent's hand like it was made of gold. If Dexter didn't do something Mr Jones was going to lose a whole load of his precious herbs and spices. Again!

Dexter cleared his throat loudly. The whole table turned round, but of course there was no one there. As they settled back down the cat waved to get Jones's attention, nodding emphatically towards the pot as if to say, *Go on! Go for it!* The cook frowned. He kept looking from his cards to the cat and back to his cards, Dexter urging him to go for it every time the man looked his way.

Mr Jones selected a couple of packets of spice and looked up at Dexter. The cat made a rolling motion with one of his paws. Mr Jones selected a couple more. Dexter rolled his paw again. Mr Jones added one more packet to the group and tossed them on the pile.

Dexter smiled when he saw the face of the *Titan's* cook drop. The man threw his cards down in disgust. "Damn you, Jonesy, when did you get so brave?"

Mr Jones swept his winnings towards him. "What can I say, boyo. Faint heart ne'er won fair lady, and all that." He glanced at Mrs Mulligan who seemed to blush as she suddenly took great interest in her own ever-growing pile of herbs and spices.

Agnes chose her words carefully. A friendly policeman was still a policeman. "My associate and I have been asked to find out what's going on with these so-called sky pirates. Who they are, what they're up to, that kind of thing. Is that something you can help us out with?"

Constable Kent also chose his words carefully. To a policeman, being open and honest worked best if the other person was the one doing most of the talking, not the other way round. "Maybe, although I think you'll find the situation is a bit more complicated than you think. Tell me, are you familiar with the history of the Lake District, Miss Dexter?"

"Should I be?"

"Not really. But it is rather fascinating. You see back in the day – I'm talking thirteenth to seventeenth century – you had England, Scotland, and this bit in the middle where you didn't go without lots of weapons and ten of your biggest mates called the Northern Marches. These lands, which included most of the Lakes, were literally a law unto themselves. They had their own traditions, their own rules, and a local sheriff whose job it was to keep the peace, although how he managed to do that I've no idea.

"The Northern Marches were home to the Border Reivers, dozens upon dozens of families and clans most of whom hated each other's guts. A feud could start over nothing and go on for centuries, and a clan wouldn't think twice about heading over the border at night to raid a rival clan, only for the other clan to do the same to them a week later. Reiving was a way of life for these people, and it's not something some of them are all that keen on giving up."

"So that's what we're dealing with here, is it? The descendants of these Border Reivers engaging in what they see as their God-given right to nick stuff."

"That's one way of looking at it."

"What other way is there?"

"Well, to them it's not theft, it's simply the way life is. Someone robs from you, so you go rob from someone else. It's not personal, and it's not malicious neither. It's just business. Why do you think that boy getting bonked on the head has caused such a stir?"

"You're saying that that boy getting his eggs scrambled was an accident?"

"I'm saying that some wee lad few can put a name to gets hurt and now here you are asking questions. Even someone as dumb as your average reiver can see how that's bad for business."

"So what would you do, if you were me? How would you deal with all of this?"

"I'd go home, say I'd failed, and get on with my life."

"And if that was not an option?"

Constable Kent took a deep breath, blowing out his cheeks as he exhaled. "You ever heard of blackmail, Miss Dexter? That comes from round here. Only it's not black*mail*, it's black *meal*, in that farmers used to pay the reivers in grain to not attack their lands, because if they didn't the local clans would come and take it anyway. You get what I'm saying?"

Agnes nodded. You didn't grow up in the east end of London without recognising a protection racket when you heard one. "Unfortunately I do, Constable," she said, lost in thought. "Unfortunately I do."

The meeting of the captains was not going well. Despite a lot of talk, John had yet to learn anything new. The most Captain Pike and Captain Grant had been able to do was confirm what he'd learnt so far. They seemed determined not to provide any new information of their own. Captain Pike remained angry that there was an investigation going on at all, and Captain Grant remained determined to get into John's pants, although thankfully she had stopped rubbing her foot up and down the inside of his leg for the time being. It was all getting a bit boring. Making his excuses, John went in search of the inn's toilet.

Heading through the bar, he saw that Agnes had made a new friend. Hopefully she was having more luck than he was. He didn't see Dexter anywhere, but he did notice that Mr Jones appeared to be having a good night, judging by the pile of paper packets that he had built up in front of him. At least someone was making out tonight.

As he headed back to the captains' meeting, John came across Mick the Spanner by the back door of the inn, talking quietly to a young woman with a mop and bucket. Mick passed the young woman something, the two of them spotting John as they made the exchange. The maid disappeared into the ladies' lounge, Mick giving John an uncertain look as he walked down the corridor towards him.

"Alright. I was just, er, seeing to a bit of laundry. For the morning, like."

John didn't remember seeing any laundry. He did remember seeing a married man and an attractive woman standing a lot closer to one another than some people might have considered entirely appropriate. "What were you getting washed? A hankie?"

Mick glanced at his empty hands. "What? Oh, er, no. No, that was just a little something to make sure we get seen to in time." He smiled awkwardly. "A little grease to smooth the action, if you know what I mean?"

"Oh, absolutely," said John, nodding sagely. "A man's gotta do what he's gotta do to get his needs taken care of, eh?"

"I guess," said Mick, smiling uncertainly. Turning on his heel, he hurried out into the night.

Returning to his meeting, John wondered what it would take to grease his own particular squeaky wheels. And if it would be worth it, even if he did.

Unfortunately for John, the second round of talks didn't prove any more productive than the first, plagued as they were by a lot of bickering, back-biting, and general all-round bitchiness. He was relieved when Captain Tonbo suggested he go back to the bar, so they could talk amongst themselves for a while. After an hour of Pike's indignation, Grant's insinuation, and Tonbo's exasperation, he was in need of a drink.

John walked into the bar to find it a lot quieter than before. The farmers had left, taking their dog and sheep with them, as had both the policeman and the guy at the bar who'd been playing Happy Families. The little girl remained though, as did the woman playing cards, both of whom John assumed belonged to the inn in some capacity since neither of them seemed worried about getting down the mountain before the werewolves got them (being this far from a major city there *had* to be werewolves or something running about out there, right?). Perhaps the woman was married to Michael, the owner, and the girl at the bar was their daughter or something.

A lot of the airship people had left too. There were a few still at the big table, determined to drink the night away, but the three bosuns were gone, as were the cooks from the other two ships.

Agnes remained also. When she saw John emerge, she moved quickly to join him by the bar. "How did it go?"

"Not very well. Captain Pike and Captain Grant are not the most helpful of people. I got the distinct impression they'd rather the see the back of me than have me sticking my nose into their business." *Or, in Captain Grant's case, another part of me entirely,* thought John.

"Well I wouldn't worry about it too much if I were you. Your little confab gave me the chance to chat with someone who had a lot to say on the matter of pirates and piracy."

"Yes, I saw you making friends with the local law. Have to say, it took me by surprise. Never thought I'd see you cosying up to one of the boys in blue. You must be going soft in your old age."

"A man shows respect he gets respect back," said Agnes. "The clothes he's got on don't matter either way to me."

"I hope you didn't give too much away about what we're up to up here."

Agnes chuckled. "I wouldn't worry about that, mate. The cat was out of the bag on you the minute you and the three captains snuck off round back together."

"No. Really?"

"Yup. They may not know exactly what you're up to, but everyone here knows you ain't no cabin boy."

John shrugged. "Ah well. Couldn't last forever. So what did Policeman Pat have to say for himself?" Agnes filled John in on what she'd learnt and his heart sank. "Well that's lovely," he grumbled. "Robber clans, of all things. So what're we meant to do about that then?"

"Pay 'em off or kill 'em," said Agnes. "Coz they ain't gonna stop just because you say please."

"Bloody hell, Agnes. That's a bit harsh innit?"

"It is what it is, Sinister," said Agnes, standing tall and stretching. "Right, I'm on watch in a few hours so I'm off to bed. See you later, Johnny Boy. Don't stay up too late now, y'hear."

Agnes left the inn, leaving John with a lot to think about. He leant on the bar, trying to figure out how you deal with a culture of theft and reprisal that had been a part of people's lives for the last six centuries or so.

Glancing down the bar, he spotted the little girl watching him, looking over then looking away like she was scared to make eye contact. John waved, but it only made things worse.

There was a pencil next to a notepad on the bar. John picked it up, examining it like it was the most fascinating thing in the world. He held it up next to his ear, rolling it between his fingers to see what sound it made. Then he sniffed it, looking surprised at how delightful it was. Checking out the side of his eye that he had the little girl's full attention, John snorted the pencil up his nose, pulling a disgusted face like it was the worst thing he had ever tasted. He sneezed, the pencil appearing in his mouth. He examined it again, unsure what to make of it. Then he nibbled down on the end, munching his way along until all of the pencil was gone again. He turned to the little girl and made an 'ugh, that was horrible' face. She didn't react, but she didn't look away either. Fiddling about in his ear he produced the pencil once more, appearing none too happy as he dragged it out the hole on the side of his head.

Setting the pencil down on the bar, he stared at it as if it was the pencil that was crazy and not him. He turned to the little girl and raised an eyebrow, hoping she had an explanation for what just happened. She didn't, but she did smile, which absolutely made John's day. All of a sudden, all those hours practising his sleight of hand hadn't been a complete waste of time after all.

The maid John had seen talking to Mick earlier appeared beside the little girl. Gathering up her things she led the girl out of the bar,

John waving goodbye as they walked off and getting a little wave back in return.

"You should count yourself lucky," said the innkeeper, coming to stand next to John. "I can't remember the last time I saw that one smile at anyone."

"Really? Does she not like strangers or something?"

"Not so much. She's deaf, y'see. Lost her hearing when her and her family got sick. It made her kind of withdrawn around people she don't know."

"Oh no," said John, looking at the girl's empty seat. "I'm sorry to hear that."

"Could've been worse. Whatever it was she had killed both her parents."

"Oh. So is the maid not her mother then?"

"No. She's just taken her under her wing, so to speak. Looking out for her until she can fend for herself."

"Well that's nice," said John.

Michael the innkeeper shrugged. "I guess." He started tidying up behind the bar. "So, Mr Cabin Boy, what can I get you?"

The way he said 'Cabin Boy' confirmed for John that what Agnes had said earlier was right, his cover was pretty much blown. "To drink, nothing. But I'll take some information if you've got any going spare?"

"Maybe I do and maybe I don't," said Michael. "Whaddaya want to know?"

"What do you know about these sky pirates you have here abouts?"

"Know about 'em? Not much. That is to say, I've heard tell there's some about, but I ain't never met any me'self."

"So you wouldn't know where I might find any?"

Michael laughed. "Up in the sky? That's the only place I know they hang out."

John decided to change tack. "What can you tell me about the Border Reivers? I hear they're still active in these parts."

"Well now, someone's been reading their history books. We haven't had any reivers round here since God knows when. All that stuff went out the window years ago. We're all good, honest, taxpaying folks these days." Michael winked at John. "Most of the time."

"So you don't think these reivers could have anything to do with the sky pirates then?"

Michael squinted at John suspiciously. "You're very interested in sky pirates for someone who says he's just a cabin boy."

"What can I say? I've always liked pirates. Didn't you ever read pirate stories when you were a kid?"

"Can't say that I did."

"Well you're missing out," said John, suddenly realising it was entirely possible Michael couldn't read.

"Looks like your boy Mento Jones is doing alright for himself for once," said Michael, nodding over at the ongoing card game. "Normally Mrs Mulligan would've cleaned him out by now."

"Sorry. Who?"

"Jones. Mento Jones. What, you mean you haven't met 'Mento' Jones yet?" Michael chuckled. "Oh boy, are you in for a treat."

"What do you mean? I don't—"

Their meeting over, the three airship captains appeared back in the bar.

Captain Pike marched into the room with a face like thunder. He stomped his way out into the night, the remainder of the *Titan's* crew tripping over themselves to rush out after him. They knew when their time was up. Captain Grant strolled out next, an amused look on her face. Walking over to John, she bent down to whisper something in his ear, taking the chance to squeeze his thigh as she did so. John blushed as she turned and headed for the door, trying not to check out the cut of her jib as she walked away (and failing miserably). And as for Captain Tonbo, she was clearly unimpressed by anything that had gone on that evening. With not a word to anyone, she left, leaving John to wonder what had happened, and what his next move should be (other than possibly taking Captain Grant up on her offer, that is).

At the poker table, Mr Jones was doing very well for himself. With Dexter's help, he'd amassed quite a pile of herbs and spices, taking not only all of Mrs Mulligan's winnings, but quite a large part of her original stake as well.

"I have to say, Jonathan, I haven't seen you play this well in, well, ever. What gives? Two dill."

Mr Jones shrugged. "Must be my guardian angel watching over me," he said, glancing up at Dexter. "Making sure I don't do nothing stupid, like. I see your dill, and raise you a nutmeg."

"Well, whatever it is, it's working," said Mrs Mulligan, sizing up her meagre pile of packets. "At this rate I'm going to struggle to make my roast tomorrow. Two coriander."

"Don't say that, Mrs M," said Mr Jones. "Your roasts are the stuff of legend. Two coriander and a fenugreek."

"Sadly, I suspect tomorrow's roast'll be the stuff of nothing much at all, not unless I get very lucky indeed. Three paprika."

"Now that would be a shame," said Mr Jones. "Three paprika and..." He pulled a special packet out from the back of the box. "And some star anise."

Mrs Mulligan was taken aback. "You *are* confident, aren't you? I don't think I've ever seen this side of you before."

"What can I say? I had to get lucky eventually," said Mr Jones, glancing up at Dexter. The cat pinched his nose and shook his head, indicating that whatever Mrs Mulligan had in her hand he thought Mr Jones could beat it.

Mrs Mulligan, however, seemed to think otherwise. "All in," she said, pushing the remains of her spices into the pot. "And there's some saffron in there an' all, so that ain't no piddlin' bet neither."

Mr Jones considered his hand. A full house, aces high. It was a risk, but it was a risk worth taking. "Call," he said, closing the lid on his little wooden box and shoving it forward.

Mrs Mulligan did her best to look like that's exactly what she had hoped for. She lay down her cards. "Two pair, aces and eights." Dexter smiled.

"Damn it," said Mr Jones, being careful to throw his cards face down on the table. "You got me. Well done, Mrs M. The pot's all yours."

Mrs Mulligan clapped her hands in glee, apologising to Mr Jones as she gathered up her winnings. Mr Jones reassured her it was fine, studiously avoiding looking up at Dexter who was still trying to work out what the hell just happened. "But there's all this cayenne and cardamon," said Mrs Mulligan. "I feel bad taking all your good spices like this. However will you manage?"

"Oh, don't worry about me, good girl. I'll get by," said Mr Jones. He swallowed nervously. "However, if you feels *really* bad about it. .. Carole, then maybe yous could, like, buy me a drink or something. To, like, y'know, make up for it, like. Or something?"

Mrs Mulligan blushed, even as she smiled back at Mr Jones. "Why, Jonathan. It'd be my pleasure."

Mr Jones beamed with delight, whilst up on the shelf Dexter shook his head slowly. *Stupid meat-sacks,* he grumbled. *Always thinking with the wrong part of their anatomy. No wonder the world's gone to hell. Honestly, if I had my way...*

Dexter's plan's for the world continued in his head whilst Mr Jones and Mrs Mulligan repaired to the bar for a little late-night aperitif (although quite what they were aperitifing was yet to be decided).

CHAPTER 4

NORTH OF THE BORDER

Agnes Goodenough stood on the deck of the *Dragonfly*, drinking in the view. For someone who grew up in the grimiest part of an already grimy city, dawn over the Lake District was a sight to behold. If only her mother could have been there to see it.

There was a battered shortbread tin that sat on a shelf in her mother's kitchen. She'd had it since she was a little girl. It was decorated with what Agnes had been told was a typical Lake District scene, that of some white-faced sheep with black and grey wool standing in a lush green field, next to a sparkling blue lake surrounded by hills and mountains. Agnes had always thought it was made up, some fantastical idea of an idyllic country scene, but standing here now, with the entirety of the Lake District spread out before her, she had no problem believing that such a view existed somewhere down below. Hell, there was probably one around every corner!

Agnes wanted her mother there because she was sure it was that biscuit tin, as much as anything else, that had convinced her to leave Nigeria in search of a better life. She'd often wondered, in all of her years stuck in the east end of London, whether her mother had ever regretted that decision. It wasn't her fault the opportunities she'd gone in search of simply did not exist, that the subjects of the empire were not as welcome in the motherland as she'd been told they would be, or that those who were born to a better life would always have a head start on those who were born with nothing. She'd made the best of what she had, made a life for herself and her family, and although it had been a struggle sometimes, Agnes couldn't remember a time when they'd been forced to go without.

But even so, she would sometimes catch her mother looking wistfully at that old battered tin and wonder what she was thinking. Was it of home, of the land she'd left behind? Or did she still dream of that ideal life, hoping it was still out there somewhere waiting for her to come find it?

Agnes resolved there and then to bring her mother up to the Lakes the first chance she got. She would also have to bring Jane and Emily up as well, for a well-deserved holiday (At the same time maybe? Now wouldn't *that* put the cat among the pigeons).

Maybe they did donkey tours, like on the beaches down Bognor way. There were some donkeys out the back of the Striding Edge, in a makeshift corral made out of some long poles stuck randomly into four big piles of hay. Perhaps they were for hire, although whether you would want to was another matter. They had a touch of the Eeyore about them, their get up and go having got up and gone. Any one of them could have walked out of there if they had wanted to, there was nothing stopping them, yet they seemed content to just lay around in the mud munching on hay, waiting for whatever humiliation life decided to throw at them next. It was sad to see, although Agnes had to admit, she knew plenty of people who were the exact same way.

A figure climbed over the side of the *Lickety Split* and stumbled down its gangplank, tucking in their shirt as they made their way over towards the *Dragonfly*. Agnes chuckled. John came up the gangplank to be greeted by the most triumphant smile he'd seen in a long time. "And where have you been?" said Agnes.

John's mind went blank. "I was, um—" He gestured vaguely at some kind of explanation somewhere over there. Agnes smiled even wider.

"So how was it?"

"How was what?"

"You know."

John adjusted himself without thinking and Agnes burst into laughter. "Oh sod off," he said, turning bright red.

Agnes batted John playfully in the chest with the back of her hand, nearly knocking the wind out of him. "Good on you, Johnny Boy. You've got to take your chances when they come. Lord knows they're few and far between."

"Ain't that the truth," mumbled John, rubbing his chest when Agnes's back was turned.

The back door of the inn opened and the little girl came tottering out clutching a bunch of carrots by their long green stalks. At the sight of her, all of the donkeys leapt to their feet – or what approximated to leaping to their feet for this group of sad sacks – and lined up along one side of the corral. In absolute earnest, the little girl went along the line of donkeys feeding each one a carrot and giving it a pat on the nose, every donkey bowing its head when she came near to receive her tiny blessing. Only when she had fed all the donkeys did the little girl realise she was being watched.

John waved and got a little half-wave in return. The back door of the inn opened and the maid emerged, carrying a wicker basket in one hand and the little girl's coat in the other. Wrapping up the child nice and warm, she glanced over at the two figures on the *Dragonfly* before leading her off back down the mountain.

"Friend of yours?" said Agnes.

"Sort of," said John.

The back door of the inn opened for a third time and a man crept out clutching his jacket and a half-eaten pie. He looked pretty pleased with himself, until he spotted John and Agnes watching him. Mr Jones walked over to the *Dragonfly*, messily finishing off his breakfast as he struggled clumsily into his crumpled jacket. Climbing over the side of the airship he, like John, was greeted by a couple of grins that he'd rather had not been there at all.

"Morning, Mr Jones," said Agnes.

"Morning."

"How was the game last night? Get lucky did we?"

"Something like that," said Mr Jones, avoiding eye contact. He turned to John. "That cat of yours around?"

"Oh, um..."

Agnes chuckled. "He wouldn't know. He only just got back himself."

Mr Jones raised an eyebrow. "Oh really?"

"Yeah," said John.

"It seems quite a night was had by all," said Agnes. John and Mr Jones exchanged a Look.

"We'll talk later," said Jones. "But for now I needs me beauty sleep."

"I'll bet you do," said Agnes.

Mr Jones went below deck.

"I should get some shut-eye as well," said John. "I'm knackered." He headed for the stairs, only to run into Captain Tonbo on her way up.

"Ah, Mr Sinister. Excellent. I was looking for you. Can you relieve Miss Dexter whilst she gets some rest. She has been up most of the night."

"What? But I was– That is to say—" Captain Tonbo frowned. "Yes, Captain. Of course, Captain. I'd be happy to."

Agnes clapped John on the back with obvious glee. "Cheers, John. See you in a few hours."

"Fantastic," John moaned. "Sleep tight."

"Oh I will," said Agnes. "Don't you worry about that."

Everyone agreed that Mrs Mulligan's roast that Sunday morning was an absolute triumph. They assumed that she'd been up all night tenderising the meat, which would explain the bags under her eyes, but whenever anyone questioned her about it she would turn red and run away, so whatever she'd done to make the meat so melt-in-your-mouth delicious would have to remain a mystery for now.

In the back room of the Striding Edge, a grim little man with all the charm of a scuffed knee sat drumming his fingers on the dining room table, watched by a fatherly-looking fellow in a flat cap who was bored out of his easy-going mind. The inn's maid was sat between them, her arms folded, trying her best to keep her temper and failing miserably.

Throwing the door open, Michael the innkeeper entered the room, taking his place at what he thought of as the head of the mostly round table. "Sorry to keep you waiting. The inn's not usually this busy on a Sunday. It seems word has gotten out about Mrs Mulligan's roast."

"Wot's this about, Fenris?" growled the grim little man. "What've you dragged us up here for?"

"I've summoned you here, Little Neck, because there is something we need to discuss."

"Summoned us?" said the fatherly fellow. "That's funny, because I don't remember getting no summonses. I remember an invitation to come and speak with the heads of the other clans, but I don't remember nothing about no summons or owt."

Fenris Wolf looked like he wanted to punch something "Forgive me, Shapside Stan. A poor choice of words on my part."

Shapside Stan waved it off as if it were nothing, tossing Molly a quick wink as he did so. Despite how angry she was, Molly had to bite her lip to keep from smiling.

"Anyway, like I was saying, there's something that we need to talk about. In short, we need to discuss the future of the Lakeland clans." Molly Sigurdsson exchanged a glance with Shapside Stan, whilst Little Neck sat up in his chair, suddenly all ears. "You all know times've been tough. Takes are down, we don't get nearly as many airships through as we used to, and now, what with this investigation going on..."

"An investigation!" squeaked Little Neck. "What kind of an investigation?"

"Just some city boy up from Hammersmyth," said Molly. "Came in last night with his girlfriend asking all sorts of stupid questions about pirates and airships and the like. I wouldn't worry about it. I don't think he got owt useful, far as I could tell."

"Oh but it *is* something to worry about," said Fenris. "This investigation represents something new from the Air Couriers Guild, a determination by them to put an end to our way of life."

"I think that's over-stating it a little, don't you, Fenris?"

"I don't, Molly, no. The air couriers are getting organised, so we need to do the same."

"Oh yes," said Shapside Stan. "And how do you suggest we do that exactly?"

"The four clans have always done things their own way. The Long Souths,"—he gestured towards Little Neck of Ecclefechan—"control the southern skies, with their harpoons and grappling hooks, whilst the Western Riders and the Northern Wolves,"—Fenris indicated Molly and himself—"have taken to the skies via airship, to ply our stock and trade."

"And how's that working out for you?" said Shapside Stan.

Fenris ignored him. "And as for the Defenders of the Western March, your command of the highways and byways is legendary, although I'm sure even you will have been feeling the pinch recently, have you not?"

Shapside Stan said nothing.

"I know I have," said Little Neck. "We don't get nuthin' round our way these days. My lads're on bread and water, and have been for a while now. If we don't sort something out soon we's gonna have to look at other ways to line our pockets." He glanced at the other clan leaders like he was wondering what they had in their pockets right now.

"The point is, trade is down," said Fenris. "There's not as much to go around, so we can't go about robbin' folk willy nilly no more. We needs to get organised."

Molly Sigurdsson snorted. "Oh yes. Organised how, exactly?"

Fenris Wolf shrugged. "Well, if one of us was to take charge, co-ordinate things as it were, we would all—"

"Ha! I knew it. He's trying to take control of the clans."

"That's not what this is about," said Fenris.

"What is it about then?"

"It's about making sure everybody gets their fair share, that's all."

"Seems like everybody gets their fair share already," said Shapside Stan.

"That's easy fer you to say," said Little Neck. "The two of yous is doing alright still. But wot about me an' Fenris, eh? 'Ow're we supposed to make a livin'?"

"That's your problem, Little Neck, not mine. I don't see why the Long Souths should get a cut of the Defenders' profits when they've done nothing to earn 'em."

"We could always come an' take our cut if ya like?" growled Little Neck.

Shapside Stan fixed Little Neck with a steady gaze. "You could try."

"Gentlemen, please," said Fenris. "We can talk about this without any unpleasantness, can't we?"

"Why?" said Molly.

"Why what?" said Fenris.

"Why do you want to talk about this now and not before? What's the rush?"

"I just think it's time we got organised, is all. For the benefit of all concerned."

Molly laughed. "And it's got nothing to do with the *Dauntless* going down in flames, I'll bet."

"She did not go down in flames," said Fenris flatly.

"No, but that's how she ended up, isn't it?" said Molly. "Funny how you were all 'every man for themselves' when you could take your pick of the choice jobs that came through, leaving the scraps for the Western Riders to go after, but now the boot's on the other foot you're all hugs and kisses and everyone gets a fair share."

"I only want to do what's right," said Fenris.

"What's right for the Wolves, y'mean. We all know where your priorities lie. They start and end with Fenris Wolf, and the rest of the world be damned. And now you want us to work together 'for the greater good'. Do me a favour. How stupid do you think we are?"

It was a hard slog up the length of Scotland for the crew of the *Dragonfly*. They had to tack their way up country, making constant adjustments to the ship in a desperate search for headway against the relentless wind. It took them three hours to reach the Dog Bone, the forty-mile ribbon of heavy industry that ran from Glasgow to Edinburgh, where it became apparent (even to someone as geographically challenged as John) that they had little chance of reaching their destination before nightfall.

There was no time to admire the heather-covered highlands and silvery lochs as they rolled by below, nor to take in the majestic sight of Ben Nevis as they swung around its enormous mass on their slow journey north. Just enough to lift their heads and mutter, "Now ain't that something," before getting back down to work, the blisters on their hands and the progress of the ship being far more pressing than stopping to wax lyrical about the mesmerising beauty of the kingdom's highest peak.

The meeting of the chiefs ended as it was always going to, with threats and recriminations over past and present slights, both real and imaginary, and with Little Neck of Ecclefechan storming out in a blind rage, promising them all some kind of reckoning that was going to happen somehow, in some way, at some time in the near future, "You mark my words!" As threats went, it wasn't the best Molly had ever been on the receiving end of.

Shapside Stan followed Little Neck out into the bar, but as Molly went to leave she found Fenris standing in her way. Molly's hand fell next to the knife she had tucked in the back of her waistline.

"May I have a word, Molly? There is something I would like to discuss."

Molly kept her hand where it was. "Go on then."

"Can we sit?" Fenris pulled out a chair. "It's about Toby."

Molly sat reluctantly. "Don't you mean Skull?"

"Yes, well…" Fenris sighed. "Look, Toby's a good lad. His heart's in the right place, even if he does have some daft ideas about names and that. All he needs is a guiding hand to keep him heading in the right direction. Do you know what I mean?"

"I guess so," said Molly, somewhat confused.

"And I've done what I can since his mother died. But he needs more than I can give him. He needs someone who can help make something of his life. Someone who can nudge him in the right direction when he goes astray. A guiding hand, if you will."

Molly frowned. "Fenris, I can't take Toby on as an apprentice. I've got enough on keeping my lot in the air as it is."

"No, you don't understand. I'm not looking to apprentice Toby. I'm looking to marry him off."

Molly's mouth fell open. "Marry! You mean, as in… me?! Like, him and me? Me and him? Together, forever?"

"Now don't say no right away. I understand this is a little unexpected. Just think about it, please. If you do I'm sure you'll see that it is an arrangement that could benefit the both of you greatly." Fenris stood. "I have to get back to work. Let's talk in a few days. You can let me know your decision then."

Molly said nothing as he left the room. She sat gaping at the wall, trying to figure out what the hell just happened, and why the hell it had just happened to her?

Molly stumbled into the main bar. She looked around for Shapside Stan, hoping to have a quiet word, but he seemed to have taken his leave. Little Neck was still there though, deep in conversation with young Toby on the other side of the room, their heads close as they discussed something of great importance.

They fell silent when Molly walked in, looking away as if the other wasn't there. Clearly they were up to no good, but Molly couldn't deal with that right now. She needed to be elsewhere before she did something she might regret, like punching stupid Toby in his stupid face until he was completely and utterly stupid bloody dead... stupid.

Stashing her maid's outfit behind the bar, she headed for the door, ignoring Fenris as he bid her goodbye, and missing completely the look he gave her as the door slammed shut behind her.

The *Dragonfly* reached its destination shortly before the sun went down, which was lucky, because securing the ship when there are no port-hooks and no one on the ground to help you is hard enough without it being pitch black at the same time. Thankfully the wind had died away, so they were able to bring her in with the minimum of fuss. Considering where they were, and what the weather was normally like, it could have been much, much worse. Subject to the ravages of the harsh Norwegian sea, Tongue, on the northern edge of the Scottish coast, was a flat, desolate place devoid of wall, hill, rock, and tree. There was nowhere to hide if the devil was after you, and nothing to stop the wind if it decided to make your life miserable just for a laugh.

They tied their ship up next to the only two buildings for miles around, a large former summer house so ill-placed it gave the word folly a whole new meaning, and a great domed something-or-other made out of iron struts and triangular panes that looked like a giant insect eye watching them as they came in to land.

"We need not rush getting her unloaded," said Captain Tonbo, as Mr Jackson lowered the gangplank. "We will be here for a few hours. I want to time our return so that we cross the Lake District when the sun is up. Tell Mr Jones there will be plenty of time for him to make something nice for supper." She glanced towards the summer house, where a woman in a brown hooded robe was hurrying towards them, an excited look on her round cheery face. "On second thoughts, we better unload everything now. I do not think that they will be willing to wait."

"You're here!" exclaimed the woman as she struggled up the gangplank. "How wonderful. We were beginning to think something had gone wrong."

"The wind was against us," said Captain Tonbo. "Our apologies for being so late."

"Oh, no matter, no matter. So long as you're all safe and sound. Everything *is* all safe and sound, isn't it?"

"Your cargo is quite secure, I assure you."

The woman clasped her hands together in delight. "Wonderful! Just wonderful. If you could put everything in the laboratory,"—she pointed at the big glass dome—"that would be super!"

John and Agnes unloaded the cargo whilst Jacko supervised loudly from afar. The boxes were so light, Agnes could have carried them by herself, one under each arm even, but for appearances sake they thought that four hands per box and taking their time was the right way to go.

Inside the great glass dome, a series of wooden panels had been built around its circumference, each with a grid of metal fixings screwed across their entire surface at regularly spaced intervals. As John and Agnes brought in each box, their client, the science monk, set about affixing their contents to the wooden panels, building up row upon row of glass balls about the size of a small grapefruit, each containing what looked like a metal windmill attached to a simple clockwork mechanism.

Eventually, John's curiosity got the better of him. "So what *are* these things anyway?"

Intent on the task at hand, the science monk had to gather her thoughts before answering. "These? These are phlogiston collectors. Are you familiar with the theory of phlogiston?" John shook his head.

"I am," said Agnes. "They used to think phlogiston was the thing that makes things burn, right? That wood had a lot of phlogiston because it burns a lot, but rock had very little because it doesn't burn at all."

"Exactly!" the science monk exclaimed.

"But I thought the phlogiston theory had been debunked, that it wasn't a real thing after all."

"Oh no, not at all. I mean, yes, kind of, but also no, if you see what I mean?" John and Agnes did not. "It's like this, you see. Phlogiston is real, but it's not the thing that makes things burn. What it is, is... it's more of a... a life force. An essence, if you will. And it's everywhere! From the tiniest little acorn to the entire Atlantic ocean. Everything has it, some things more than others, and if we can harness that energy, direct it where we want it to go, we can achieve anything!"

"So that's what these little doodads are about then?" said John. "They're phlogiston collectors."

"Precisely. They gather up the phlogiston in their little vortices, and this allows us to access the phlogiston directly."

"To do what exactly?" asked Agnes.

The science monk laughed, somewhat maniacally. "Whatever we want!"

John considered the many panels they'd built around the room. Whatever they planned on doing with this phlogiston stuff, they seemed to need a lot of it. "Is phlogiston dangerous?"

The science monk gave an all too casual shrug. "There is a certain amount of risk involved, as with any scientific discovery, but I'm certain that with the proper precautions we can achieve our goal."

"Which is what, exactly?"

"Well—" The door to the lab opened and an old man in a brown robe wandered in clutching a sandwich and a cup of tea. "Oh! Sir! Look. The collectors are here. Aren't they wonderful!"

The old man shuffled up to the nearest panel to inspect the delivery, munching on his sandwich as he took in the collectors' every detail. "Yes. Good. Very good. These will do nicely. Well done, my dear. This is fine work, fine work indeed. I cannot wait to see them in action."

"Well, sir, if we work together to get them all fixed and aligned, I'm sure we could be ready to begin within the hour. There are rather a lot of them, and I—" But the old man was already shuffling back out of the laboratory door, slurping noisily on his tea as he went.

The woman sighed as she watched him leave. "My colleague is a genius, truly he is, but he does have his little eccentricities."

"Like what? Leaving all the work to other people?" said Agnes. "Oh yeah, I'm familiar with that kind of 'eccentricity' alright."

John and Dexter sat in the *Dragonfly's* now empty hold, finishing off the last of the meal Mr Jones had painstakingly prepared. Neither of them had tried samosas with mango chutney before, but they both agreed that they were damn tasty and no mistake.

"So what did you find out at the Striding Edge?" asked John.

"You mean apart from the fact that Mr Jones is bad at poker? Not a hell of a lot. None of the crew talk I listened in on had anything nice to say about the sky pirates, if they even mentioned them at all, and all the locals seemed to care about was sheep farming and some bloke named Howie Widya."

"Howie Widya?"

"Yeah. They kept saying 'Howie Widya this' and 'Howie Widya that'. I'm telling you, whoever this guy is, they didn't seem to like him very much."

John chuckled. "I think maybe they were saying 'away wid ya'. Like 'get away with you'. As in, 'oh, bugger off'. Y'know?"

Dexter stared off into the distance. "Come to think about it, that would make more sense."

"So you didn't hear anyone saying anything that might incriminate themselves?"

"I didn't, no. Why, how did you get on?"

"Much the same really. The captains were more interested in bickering amongst themselves than telling me anything I needed to know. Not that they seemed to know anything. Whoever's passing information to the sky pirates they're keeping a very low profile."

"Which would be a smart move," said Dexter. "Although not very helpful to us."

"Indeed," said John. "Although Agnes did come up with something interesting. Have you ever heard of the Border Reivers?"

"Does it seem likely that I would have?"

John ignored him. "Well these reivers are—" They heard a noise. Looking up, they discovered Agnes standing by the hold door.

"Oy, Sinister. The captain wants to see you." Agnes walked off, back the way she'd come. John and Dexter exchanged looks.

"Do you think she heard us?" asked Dexter.

"No, I don't think so," said John, not entirely convinced. "Anyway, I better get on. Remind me to tell you about the reivers later. It's a fascinating story."

"Will do," said Dexter. "Come find me in the kitchen when you're done."

"The kitchen? You want to be careful. Jones'll have your head if he catches you trying to sneak food."

Dexter chuckled. "Oh, I think you'll find that Mr Jones and I have come to a new understanding."

On deck, John found Captain Tonbo waiting for him on the forecastle.

"Ah, Mr Sinister. Thank you for joining me. I wanted to ask how your investigation is going? Did you learn much from our visit to Striding Edge? I know the other captains were not the most helpful, but perhaps Miss Dexter had more luck amongst the locals?"

"Well, Captain, let's see." John took a moment to consider how certain he was about some of the things he'd seen. Certain enough to tell the man's wife about? Probably not. "There's definitely something dodgy going on at Striding Edge. I'm pretty sure it's where the sky pirates are getting their information, although how and from whom I don't know yet. Tell me, how long has Mr Jackson been part of the crew?"

"You suspect Mr Jackson of being involved?"

"I never rule anything out. Has he been on board long?"

"Since we first took flight. Over a year ago now."

"And you trust him completely?"

"I do. Why? Has he done something to make you believe I should not?"

"Not exactly, no. But ever since Agnes and I have been on board he's been on us like flies on"—John saw the disapproving look in Captain Tonbo's eye—"on you know what. So I figured maybe he's got something to hide. Like he doesn't want us around or something." Captain Tonbo seemed unconvinced. "And when we were in Iron Bridge he was acting all suspicious and that too."

"Suspicious how?"

"He bought some grapes, some lard, and some comic books, then he gave Dex– I mean, Miss Dexter the slip. Now I don't know where he went, I don't know if he was out to bribe someone or not, but it does make me wonder what he was up to, y'know?"

Captain Tonbo tilted her head to one side. She was used to dealing with naive yet enthusiastic cabin boys, it was part of the job, although usually they were a lot younger and slightly less naive than the one stood before her right now. "Mr Jackson may be something of a prickly customer, but he is as reliable as they come. If he has been off with you it is because he objects to my replacing our missing cabin boy so quickly. Bert, the young man in question, is his nephew. He hopes to see him back aboard the *Dragonfly* one day, as soon as he is well enough that is. His nephew is recovering from his ordeal at his mother's house, near Iron Bridge, which I believe explains the grapes and the comic books, as well as the lard. Mr Jackson is always careful to bring something of use to his sister whenever he is in town."

"Oh, I see," said John. "Yes, that does make sense. Alright then, since we're on the subject, what about Mr Jones? Do you trust him completely as well?"

"Mr Jones is the finest cook in the entire Air Couriers Guild. We are lucky to have him on board."

"Someone in Striding Edge said he had a nickname. They said people sometimes call him Mento Jones. Do you know why that is? Is that something I should know about?"

Captain Tonbo became very serious. "I would not say that name again if I were you. Mr Jones would not like it."

"Of course," said John. *Crikey. First Mick the Spanner, now Mento Jones. Does* everyone *on this ship have a name you're not allowed to use?* "But is it something I need to be concerned about?"

"It is not."

John nodded, pausing to rearrange the thoughts in his head. Captain Tonbo did not look happy. "I hope you have made enquiries beyond the bounds of this ship, Mr Sinister. I would hate to think you have spent the majority of your time investigating my crew."

"Lord no. Heaven forbid," said John quickly. "No, I've actually got a theory that might have a bit of legs. Or at least my colleague, Miss Dexter, does." John laid out what he'd learnt from Agnes about the Border Reivers. "So if you could drop me off on the way back down south I can have a little look around, see what I can come up with. If I can maybe identify these reivers, make contact with them even, I might be able to find a way to get them to leave you alone from now on."

Captain Tonbo did not seem overly impressed. "As you wish, Mr Sinister, although I cannot 'drop you off on the way', as you would like. We have a lot of money on board, which is usually when the sky pirates decide to strike. I intended to avoid the Lake District if at all possible, and should the winds blow us in its general direction I certainly do not intend to land. I can drop you near Morecambe and you can get the train back. That is the best I can do. Hopefully that is acceptable to you."

Not really, thought John, *but it'll have to do.* "Perfect," he said, smiling. "Thank you, Captain."

Magnus Sigurdsson could tell by the look on his sister's face that the meeting of the chiefs had not gone well. He didn't need to wait for her to boot a bucket across the cave floor, sending it into the deep water beneath the airship with a resounding plop.

"Well we're not getting that back again," said Magnus. "What happened?"

"What I said was going to happen. Fenris tried to take over."

"And did he?"

"No, he didn't."

"Then what are you so upset about?"

"Because when that didn't work that son of a"—Molly looked over at Sue, who was sitting next to the fire. She might not be able to hear the words, but she was surprisingly good at reading lips these days—"you know what, tried to marry me off to that idiot boy of his, like I'd be glad to take him off his hands or something."

Magnus burst out laughing. "He didn't, did he?"

"He bloody did."

"And you said no, right?"

"I didn't get a chance to! I was too shocked to say anything."

"That's understandable, I guess."

Molly slumped down onto a nearby sack of spuds. "I'm just so sick of it all. Bloody Fenris and Little Neck acting like what I want don't matter. If it weren't for Shapside Stan we'd be royally screwed, you know. Fenris would wipe us out without a second thought."

"You know what it is," said Magnus. "It's coz you work at the inn as a maid. It makes Fenris think he can tell you what to do all the time."

"I know. But what am I meant to do? If I wasn't there we'd never know about any of the good scores coming through, and neither would Fenris. Those guys up there trust me, they know I don't mess about. If we left it up to Fenris to sort out he'd mess it right up, and then where would we be? It's hard enough to make ends meet as is. I dread to think what it'd be like with *him* in charge." Molly rubbed her tired eyes. "I tell you what, I don't know how much longer we can go on like this. I reckon this whole sky piracy thing is gonna end soon enough."

"Give over," said Magnus, digging out a long pole to go bucket fishing. "We've got years to go yet." He headed over to the water's edge. "So long as no one does anything daft to spoil it all, that is."

"Exactly," said Molly, under her breath. "That's what I'm worried about."

It was late into the night before the *Dragonfly* departed Tongue on its long journey south. With an empty hold, the wind at their back, and a lockbox full of coin in the captain's cabin, the ship was as content as it was possible for an airship to be. Captain Tonbo took the wheel, leaving her crew at their leisure. They'd put some good work in these past few days, they deserved a bit of time to themselves.

John and Agnes stood on the forecastle, enjoying the quiet as they went over everything they'd learnt so far.

"The captain's going to drop me off on the way back so I can see about these reiver clans, see if I can find out what they're up to," said John. "I know it's not what we discussed regarding this job, but I'd appreciate the company if you have the time?"

"I dunno about that, Sinister. If I'm gone too long Nero might get the hump."

"I understand. How about we give it a couple of days and see. If nothing's come of it by Friday we could hop on the train back to Hammersmyth and have you back at work first thing Monday morning."

"I'll think about it," said Agnes, looking out towards the horizon.

That wasn't the answer John was looking for. "It'd give you a chance to see your friend the policeman again, get to know each other a bit better."

"I ain't friends with any policeman," said Agnes. "Just friend*ly*. There's a difference."

"Yeah? Coz I thought maybe the two of you might... y'know."

"Know what?"

"Might want to, like, get to know each other a little better. As in, 'get to know each other a little better', if you know what I mean."

Agnes turned to look at John. "Constable Kent is not my type."

"Because he's a policeman. Right, I get it."

"No, not because he's a policeman. Because he's a man."

"Oh." The look on John's face as his brain chased down that statement to its logical conclusion was almost comical. "Oh! I see. Yes, right. Got you. Not your type. I'm with you now."

"You alright, John? You look befuddled."

"No, no, not at all. It's just not something I'd ever thought about, y'know. As in, like, who you might be... y'know. And, like, who you might not want to, y'know, with."

Agnes chuckled. "I know. That's one of the things I like about you, Sinister. You've always taken me for me." Agnes looked down at her hands where they grasped the ship's side rail, suddenly nervous. "Sinister, can I ask you something? Has it ever occurred to you why me and your sister have been hanging out so much?"

"I can't say that it has. I just figured you two were friends."

"We are. Good friends. I mean, *really* good friends, if you know what I mean."

John should have known what she meant, but he was having a little trouble squaring it away in his head. "Like... bosom buddies, that kind of thing?"

Agnes burst out laughing. "That's one way of putting it, yes." As quickly as it came, the laughter went away again. "That's not a problem for you, is it?"

"What? No, not at all. Each to his own, and all that. I mean, *her* own, I mean. But I—"

"But what?"

"I didn't know Jane felt that way about... y'know. I mean, she was engaged to be married once. To a man, and everything."

"And look how well that turned out."

Lots of shouting and an acrimonious split when she was six months gone with little Emily, that's how. "You make a good point."

Agnes kept her eyes firmly fixed on the horizon. "I hope you can get on board with this, John, because I really like Jane, and she really likes me, I think, but she's having a hard time coming to terms with it all. If it turned out you had a problem with it that could be the end for us, y'know."

For a moment, John thought he saw real fear in Agnes's eye. "Hey, listen," he said. "I got no problem with it. Far as I'm concerned, so long as everyone's happy, it's got nothing to do with me."

"That's fair enough, I guess," said Agnes. It wasn't quite the answer she'd been looking for either.

John joined Agnes in contemplating the horizon, standing in silence until he decided to show her how normal everything still was between them by awkwardly changing the subject. "So what about that lot back there, with their phlogiston collectors. Do you think this experiment of theirs has got a hope in hell?"

"Well, considering they're basing it all on a defunct theory that didn't work in the first place, I'd put their chances at somewhere between no way and you must be crazy."

As if on cue, a faint glow appeared on the horizon behind them. It pulsed a strange wibbly colour that John could only describe as glurple, growing brighter as it lit up the night sky. There was an accompanying hum that vibrated in John's stomach, threatening its contents with making a sudden reappearance (although which end they planned on using as an exit was still up for grabs) until, with a pop, the sound was gone, the light vanished, and the only evidence that remained of its existence was the feeling that he should use the head sooner rather than later, just to be on the safe side.

"I guess their experiment worked," said Agnes.

"I guess so."

Agnes placed a hand on her stomach. "Do you need the loo?"

"I think I do, yes."

"Um... do you mind if I go first?"

"No," said John. "But be quick about it. I'm not sure how much longer I can hold out."

"Oh don't worry," said Agnes, hurrying off. "I don't think speed is going to be an issue."

It had been a long day at the Striding Edge. The now legendary roast dinner had given way to a full day of epic drinking, which would lead to a great many astounding hangovers in the morning. There was plenty of cleaning to be done, and an unbelievable amount of washing up, but that was fine with young Toby Wolf. As far as he was concerned a bad day in the kitchen was better than a good day freezing your you-know-what's off on the deck of an airship any day of the week.

"Hey, boy. C'mere," his father called from over by the bar.

"Yes, Dad?" Fenris glowered at him. "I mean, yes, boss?"

"Did you talk to Little Neck like I asked?"

"I did."

"And? What did he say?"

Toby swallowed loudly. "He said that anything that lines his pockets is alright by him." *He also said that if Fenris reckons he's in charge from now on he can kiss my hairy backside*, thought Toby, although he wisely decided to keep that bit to himself.

"Good, good," said Fenris. "So we can count on his help against the Riders?"

"I think so, yes."

Fenris glared down at his son. "Don't 'think', boy, you're not good at it. Is he in or isn't he?" Toby nodded silently. "Right then." Fenris turned away.

"Um, boss? What is the plan now anyway? What *are* we going to do?"

Fenris grinned. "Whatever we want," he said, heading out from behind the bar. "You can finish up here, I reckon. I'm going to bed. Try not to burn the place down before you leave."

"Yes, boss. Of course, boss. No problem, boss," said Toby glumly.

Chapter 5

In The Drink And Up The Creek

The *Dragonfly* reached the Lakes at dawn. Dark clouds had gathered, turning the land as flat and grey as a pile of soggy old newsprint. John stood on the prow of the ship, trying to work out if they were about to get drenched or not, when he was joined by Captain Tonbo.

"Do we need to stand watch like last time?" he asked.

"No. They will not attack when we are this high. They know we would see them coming and make a run for it before they got anywhere near."

"Really? So it's safer this way? How come we didn't do this before? Why did we fly in so low?"

"Sky at night is blue. We are not. They would have seen us before we saw them."

At the helm, Mick the Spanner was eyeing up the ship's balloon, an unhappy look on his face. "Um, Captain. Can I see you for a moment?" Captain Tonbo joined her husband at the wheel. "I don't like how the balloon is looking," said Mick. "We might have a leak."

"Looks fine to me," said Captain Tonbo.

"Still, I'd prefer to land and check it out. Maybe top up at Striding Edge while we're there."

"It cannot wait?"

"Possibly, but who knows. If there is a leak, Striding Edge is our last chance to get gas before Telford. I wouldn't want to risk it."

Captain Tonbo pursed her lips. "Mr Sinister," she called. "Pass the word for Mr Jackson and Miss Dexter. It seems we must stand watch after all."

Molly Sigurdsson kicked her brother awake. "Get up, lazy arse. It's time."

"What time? Time for what?" Magnus grumbled.

"Time to get paid," said Molly, handing him his crossbow.

Molly Sigurdsson climbed aboard the *Kiss*, to see how preparations were going. Her three man crew – Snick the Cutter and the two Jacks – had been there since sunrise getting her ready for take-off. The two Jacks were on boiler duty, whilst Snick took care of the rigging. Snick wasn't built for shovelling. He was their in-and-out man. Small and scrappy, like a skinny squirrel with an eye for the shiny, Snick had a talent for getting into places he shouldn't, and taking things that didn't belong to him. Some people called it stealing. He referred to it as the forced redistribution of wealth, although it was funny how the redistribution part always seemed to start in someone else's pocket and end up in his own.

"How you doing, Snick? You ready to make some money?"

"Always, boss," said Snick, with a wink.

"Same as before, right? We keeps 'em busy whilst you do what you do best."

Snick acknowledged Molly's orders with a quick tug of the forelock.

Molly was glad Snick had stayed on when her father retired. She was glad of the two Jacks too of course, they were a good, reliable pair of bruisers (which you can never have too many of when the you-know-what hits the propellor) but a man of Snick's talents was hard to come by. Keeping the clan in clover would have been a damn sight harder if he hadn't been around.

Magnus Sigurdsson trotted up the gangplank, all decked out in his regulation raiding garb – black on black with a bit of black to finish, and a red handkerchief tied somewhere about your person so that you can tell friend from foe. "Alright! Let's do this. Time to make some money!"

Molly smiled. It was a matter of pride for the reiver clans that a man could go from bed to horse in a matter of minutes, riding full pelt into battle like he'd been working himself up to it all morning. Her brother went round the men, laughing and joking as he pumped them up for the fight to come. *He's a good man to have on your side,* thought Molly. *And a good brother to boot.* Like Snick, she wasn't sure what would have happened to the clan if he hadn't been around.

"What a ship!" exclaimed Magnus to his sister. "Look at her. I mean, look at her! Look how gorgeous she is. How ready for a fight! I can't wait! They won't know what hit 'em. I'm telling you, this is gonna be fun, eh, sis'? Waddaya say? You up for this? You ready to go to war?!"

Molly Sigurdsson drew her sword. "You're damn right I am."

As the *Dragonfly* dropped towards the Striding Edge, John caught a flash of light in the murky greyness below. He waved to Jacko who joined him at the ship's rail.

Jacko cursed with an eloquence befitting of his station. "Go tell the captain, and be quiet about it. We can't let on that we've seen 'em."

John hurried over to the captain, who took the news with a surprising amount of calm. "Well spotted, Mr Sinister. Now, if you would be so kind, my compliments to Mr Jones, and please tell him we are about to have guests for lunch."

"Guests?" said John.

The captain nodded. "He will understand. Quickly now, there is not much time."

John went below deck, nearly falling down the stairs as the ship made an unexpected sharp left turn. He found Mr Jones in the galley, contemplating a selection of root vegetables.

"Mr Jones, the captain sends her compliments, and, er, she says we're going to have guests for lunch?"

Mr Jones frowned at John. "Is that so, is it? Well now, that is annoying and no mistake." Mr Jones began unbuttoning his shirt. "My compliments to the captain, and tell her I'll be ready. Hurry now, lad! Don't dawdle. There ain't no time to waste."

As she cleared the cave, the *Molly's Kiss* swung up and to the left, angling towards the top of Helvellyn. They could see their prey coming in to the Striding Edge, a black dot against the slate-coloured sky.

Weapons in hand, her crew was silent and still, the only sound the chug of the *Kiss's* engine as the ship pushed against the prevailing wind.

Her captain drove the ship hard, more concerned with closing the gap than she was about not being seen. A daylight raid was no time to be subtle.

Emerging back into the light, John was intercepted at the top of the stairs by Jacko, the bosun shoving a long, curved blade into his hand. "What'm I supposed to do with this?" he asked, panicking a little.

Jacko sneered. "You stick 'em wiv the pointy end, don't'cha."

"But... a sword, though? I mean, ain't you got any guns?"

Jacko pointed up at the big bag of explosive gas above their heads. "What did I tell you? No flames, remember."

"Not even a pistol though?"

"*Especially* no pistols," said Jacko, walking away.

Blade in hand, John went up on the quarterdeck. "Mr Jones said, um..." *Damn! What the hell was it that he'd said?*

"Did he start taking off his shirt?" asked Captain Tonbo.

"He did."

"Then that is well enough, Mr Sinister. Now, go join Miss Dexter on the main deck. And remember, show no mercy, for you will get none in return."

"Aye, Captain," said John, a quiver in his voice.

Agnes was standing by the stump of the main mast, looking fairly unbothered by what was going on. "Where's your sword?" said John. "Did Jacko not give you one?"

"He tried," said Agnes. "But they ain't for me. I like to keep my hands empty, know what I mean?" John didn't, but he nodded anyway. Agnes smiled at him. "Relax, Sinister. It's never as bad as you think it's gonna be. Just keep your feet, keep 'em at bay, and you'll be alright in the end. Most people don't want to fight, even the ones that start something. Just show 'em you ain't to be messed with and you'll come through right enough."

"And what if they *do* want to fight?" asked John. "What then?"

"Then you kill 'em before they can kill you," said Agnes.

John looked away, wishing he was elsewhere. He spotted Dexter at the top of the stairs. The cat took one look at what was going on, shook his head, and disappeared back below deck. *Lucky sod*, thought John, wondering if anyone would notice if he went and did the same.

At Captain Tonbo's order, Mick the Spanner put the *Dragonfly's* back to the wind, adjusting her sails so that they stuck straight out from the ship's hull, as upright as a regimental sergeant major. The ship tilted forward as she picked up speed, rocketing her way south as their pursuers swung from their one o'clock to their three o'clock, eventually slipping in behind the *Dragonfly* where they started to quickly gain ground. It seemed that steam beat sail in the air, as well as on the ground.

The two ships cut between a pair of hills, dropping down into the long run along the length of Lake Windermere. Engine thumping, the pirate ship began pulling level with the *Dragonfly* on her right, where John got his first good look at her. Black from tip to tail, including her balloon, she was hard and sleek and scarred and lean, with nothing on her decks but knives, grappling hooks, and the promise of death (which amounted to the same thing). She was a mad dog spoiling for a fight, the sort of dog that you kept your eye on as you backed away slowly. Whatever happened next, it was going to hurt.

"Damn it," said Jacko, glancing from the ship on their right to the mountains to their left. "We're boxed in. I hope you two know how to fight, coz it's comin'."

"Don't you worry about us," said Agnes. "We know what's what. Right, John?"

John nodded dumbly, clinging to his sword with both hands. He felt sick.

The pirate ship drew level with the *Dragonfly*. "Stop and be boarded!" yelled her captain.

"Never!" Captain Tonbo yelled back.

"As you wish," the pirate captain replied. She swung her ship hard left, looking to smash the *Dragonfly's* wings.

"Damn it!" Mick cursed, grabbing at the ship's controls. Pulling levers and kicking open locks, he flattened the wings on the starboard side hard against the hull.

"What are you doing?" yelled Captain Tonbo.

The pirate ship smashed into the *Dragonfly*, staggering both crews. The pirates threw out grappling hooks, tying the two ships together as their pilots fought for control.

"Prepare to repel boarders!" Captain Tonbo rushed to the side. John was about to join her when he spotted something out the corner of his eye that stopped him dead in his tracks.

Mr Jones appeared on deck in nothing but his birthday suit and his old leather butcher's apron. He had on boots, and he may have had on trousers with the legs rolled up, but it was hard to tell. He had his father's meat tenderiser in his right hand, his chopping board strapped to his left forearm, and he looked as though someone had just accused him of using too much salt and they needed to pay! He also had a small sack of flour tied to his left hip, although what he planned on doing with that was anyone's guess. *Well now,* thought John. *Mento Jones, I assume.*

John joined the others at the ship's rail, where half the crew fought to free the ship whilst the other half fought to stave off the pirate horde. As quickly as they threw off one grappling hook, another took its place. The pirates seemed more concerned with keeping the two ships tied together than they were about coming aboard. They had yet to make any concerted effort to breach the deck.

Dexter made his way to the captain's cabin. He figured it was the safest place to be, all things considered. It was the only room with a lock on the door for a start.

At the front of the boat, beneath the forecastle, it was a nice room if you liked that sort of thing. Sparsely furnished, with a map-covered desk on one side and a matching pair of sea-chests on the other, the only bit that wasn't spic and span was the large double bed in between the ship's two glass eyes, which looked like it had last been used to host the national pillow fighting championships. It also looked incredibly inviting.

Jumping on the bed, Dexter nestled himself in amongst a big pile of pillows, as he waited for the attack to be over.

Glass broke overhead. Dexter looked round. A man in black was squeezing in through a small hole in one of the eyes. He had a crowbar, a knife, and he looked happy to use either of them should the need arise. Dexter ducked even deeper into the pile of pillows and watched.

The man went to the end of the bed and reached underneath. Dragging out a small iron-banded box, he plonked it down on the bed, going to work on the lock with his crowbar. He didn't have to work very hard. The box popped open with a woody crunch, giving up its contents like a gossipy neighbour who'd just been told something in the strictest confidence. The box contained a small notebook, a bag of what Dexter assumed was gold (he wasn't entirely sure what these meat-sacks held most dear, but he'd always thought gold figured into it somewhere along the line) and a literal wodge of cash. The man began counting through the cash, a big smile on his weaselly little face.

Oh no you don't, Sonny Jim, thought Dexter. *Not on my watch.*

Leaping from his hiding place, Dexter sank his teeth into the man's hand. The man squealed, waving his arm around as he stumbled around the room. He smacked into the wall, accidentally slamming Dexter hard against the woodwork. The cat fell, landing head first in a pile of dirty laundry.

Crawling out from beneath a pair of greasy overalls, Dexter spotted the thief climbing out through the broken window, the huge wodge of cash in his hand.

Growling with rage, Dexter went out after him.

On deck, the battle with the pirates appeared to be going well. Agnes, unable to reach across the gap between the two ships, had found herself a wooden stave which she was using to whack any bit of pirate that came near. Jacko and the captain had cut the number of grapples holding them together by half but they were having trouble with the last two, mainly because of Mr Mento Jones, who was striding up and down between the two ships, a foot balanced on each rail, swinging his tenderiser at anyone he wasn't on first name terms with as he threw handfuls of flour in their unsuspecting faces. A wispy pall of death hung over the scene, in the form of some weapons grade self-raising. It made swinging an axe with any kind of accuracy very difficult indeed.

And as for John, John liked to feel like he was doing his part.

One of the pirates levelled a crossbow at Mr Jones, but when he fired, the cook caught the bolt in the chopping board strapped to his arm. Screaming with rage that anyone would dare do such a thing, Mr Jones leapt onto the pirate ship, charging at the shocked pirate as he scrambled to reload.

"Damn it, Jonesy!" Jacko screamed. "Get back here. Now!" But Mr Jones wasn't listening. He knocked the crossbow out of the pirate's hand, smacked him upside the head with the tenderiser, grabbed him by the scruff of the neck, and threw him across the deck into the gap between the two ships.

The pirate tumbled into the open space, only just managing to brace himself at the last moment. Mr Jones jumped back onto the *Dragonfly*, running to grab the pirate's arms so he could drag him on board to give him a right good walloping.

"Magnus!" the pirate captain screamed, abandoning the wheel to rush to the young man's aid. Grabbing his legs, she tried to pull him free of Jones's grasp, as determined to get him back aboard as the cook was not to give up his prize. The poor pirate, dangling between the two ships with nothing but fresh air between him and the end of all ambition, could do nothing but hope they both didn't let go at the same time.

A harpoon with a head like an iron Christmas tree shot between the two ships, narrowly missing the dangling pirate, but stopping the fighting stone dead. The two crews stared at each other. Peering over the side, they discovered that the mountain below was a lot nearer than it should have been, and that it was crawling with grubby little men with swords and axes, rushing about trying to reload their massive harpoon gun before the two airships drifted out of range.

"Damn it!" Jacko cursed. "Get those lines cut. We need to get out of h—URGHH!" Jacko choked as Agnes grabbed him by the collar and flung him to the ground, seconds before a harpoon bolt shot through the air right where his head used to be. The dangling pirate squealed in terror. Jacko's head had been very near his own at the time.

"Hold on, Magnus," the pirate captain yelled, flinging her sword across the gap at Mento Jones.

The cook threw up his hands to protect his face, his half of the pirate falling into the gap between the two ships. Left dangling by his ankles, the pirate did the only thing you can do in a situation such as that; he screamed.

"Cut away! Cut away!" ordered the pirate captain as she dragged her crewman back on board. Axes flashed and the two ships surged apart, the pirates heading for open skies as the *Dragonfly* lurched towards the rocky mountainside. At the wheel, Mick the Spanner threw the ship hard a-starboard, the deck listing to the left as they turned swiftly away from almost certain death.

"We did it!" yelled John, throwing his arms up in celebration, until he realised that no one was celebrating with him. They were all looking at the balloon above their heads. He followed their gaze to find two fist-sized holes in the thing that was meant to be keeping them in the air, their ragged edges flapping frantically as the gas within rushed to escape. They weren't big holes, it would take a while to empty the balloon completely, but the ship needed to land, and she needed to land fast.

"Get us over the water," ordered Captain Tonbo. "Everybody brace for impact!"

John glanced over the side to see where the lake was only to find the ship skimming over an expanse of slate roofs and red brick chimney tops. They were over a small town, with the lake a few hundred yards away. He winced as the ship clipped someone's chimney, sending rubble into the street below. Someone yelled, although their anger was cut short when they caught sight of the airship swooping overhead.

John, a confirmed agnostic, quickly crossed himself, forgetting for a moment which way round it went. *Just get us to the lake,* he prayed. *I swear I'll be a good boy from now on. No more drinking, no more gambling, and– and– and I'll give money to charity and that. Okay? Whatever you want. Just get us to the lake, please!*

He crossed himself again as the *Dragonfly* clipped another roof, throwing him to his knees. Cowering on the floor, John waited for the inevitable, but it never came. Instead, an eerie silence descended over the ship. Risking a glance over the side, John discovered they were over water, the hoped-for soft landing rushing up to meet them at an alarming speed.

The *Dragonfly* slammed into the lake, bouncing through the waves as she fought to stay in the air. Rigging snapped as she eventually gave up hope, coming to a lurching stop in the middle of the lake, a huge bow wave surging out in front of her in a way that it had not done in many a year.

A series of cracking sounds shot around the ship, unhappy noises that didn't herald the arrival of anything good.

"Get below and shore up," the captain ordered. "Caulk and rope in every crack. Quickly now, afore she sinks."

"But won't she float?" said John. "I thought ships could float."

Pulling a pirate knife from her mechanical arm, the captain examined its mangled mechanism. "She has been dry and dangling for far too long, Mr Sinister. For her to float now would be a miracle."

Below decks it turned out the captain was right. Tiny leaks shot out all over the place, criss-crossing the hold from one side to the other. Jacko shoved a handful of scrap rope and canvas into John's hand. "You get started in here." He passed more caulk to Mr Jones and Agnes. "You two see to the galley and crews quarters." They ran off at a trot. "Shove it in tight till you can shove no more, an' be quick about it," he called after them. "We get'ny lower an' we're done for." Grabbing some caulk himself, Jacko followed Mick down a hatch into the bilge at the bottom of the ship. John heard them splashing around down there. It sounded like the water was more than ankle deep already.

John rushed around the hold jamming material into the splits in the wood with his pocket knife. It seemed like no sooner had he got one leak filled than another two appeared in its place, but slowly and surely he got them under control.

When he was halfway down the hold, Agnes appeared to give him a hand. "Crew's quarters weren't that bad. Just a few leaks," she said, taking over one side of the ship whilst John finished off the other. Working their way from front to back, they filled the last remaining holes, reaching the rear of the hold just as the caulk ran out.

Jacko and Mick climbed up out of the bilge, soaked through and exhausted. Resting with his hands on his knees, Jacko scanned the hold. "Are we done? D'ya get 'em all?" John and Agnes nodded dumbly.

Mr Jones joined them in the hold. He'd ditched the apron and chopping board, and was wearing clothes once more. "The galley's all tight an'all. We had a few big 'uns but I got 'em proper filled and that, like."

"Good, good. Well done, everyone. Now, let's grab some buckets and see about bailing out. Mr Jones, we may need some of yer big pots an'all. Can you bring us some so we can form a decent line."

Mr Jones nodded, too tired to argue. John was surprised, knowing how precious every cook was about their pots and pans. Wherever the rage monster Mento Jones had come from, he seemed to have gone away again.

The *Molly's Kiss* swung out over the lake, curving round the stricken *Dragonfly* as she ran to get clear of those that meant to do her harm. At the wheel, her captain was letting rip with every swear word she could think of, as well as inventing a few of her own when the ones she already knew started to prove lacking. "Damn Little Neck! I'm gonna kill him. I'm gonna cut him from stem to stern. I'm gonna pull his insides out. I'm gonna stomp on his liver and kick him in the kidneys. And then, AND THEN!!!– Then I'm *really* gonna start to go to town on him."

Magnus waited for his sister to stop punching the ship's wheel before daring to interrupt. "Snick got the money though," he offered. "So it turned out alright in the end."

"Barely," barked Molly, turning on her brother. "And no thanks to the Long Souths neither." Magnus simply nodded. It was safer than speaking again. "So how much did we get anyway?"

Magnus beamed. "Nearly two hundred pounds, according to Snick."

"What?! But how? That's way too much. How much did they have on board for crying out loud? Snick. Snick!" The thief, looking a bit sorry for himself, limped up the stairs to join them on the quarterdeck. "What's this I hear about two hundred pounds? Were they rich or something? You didn't take everything they had, did you?"

Snick hung his head in shame. "I'm sorry, Cap'n. I didn't mean to. I were counting out our cut when this wild beast came at me an' tried to take me 'ead off. Musta been a wolf or summink. It was all teeth and claws and that, and it near bit clear through me arm.

I was lucky to get outta there alive. An' when I did, I found I had all their money in me hand still. I never left 'em nuffink. I'm sorry, boss. I know I messed up. I feel right bad about it I do."

Molly Sigurdsson sighed. "Alright. Never mind. See to your wounds and we'll sort it out when we get back. In fact, there'll be a lot to sort out when we get back, including with Mr Fenris Wolf."

"Fenris?" said Magnus. "What's Fenris got to do with anything?"

"You don't think the Long Souths would've made a play for our score without Fenris's approval, do you? Not a chance. No, whatever the hell's going on here you can bet your almost-harpooned backside that our boy Fenris is neck deep in the whole thing. And for that,"—Molly slammed the axe she'd used to cut away the lines into the quarterdeck's guard rail, almost slicing it all the way through—"For that there's going to be a *real* reckoning."

Chapter 6

A Storm Is Brewing

The bucket line was slow going. As well as all the oddly shaped pots and pans they had to deal with, John and Agnes had to contend with the *Dragonfly's* balloon, which had deflated completely and was now lying over the ship like a dropped pancake. They'd found a few bits of wood to prop it up out of the way here and there, but still it seemed like whichever way you turned you got a load of canvas in your face.

"This can't be the best way to do this," John complained, as he splashed himself with bilge water for the thousandth time.

"Can you think of a better way?" said Agnes

"Well... no. But that doesn't mean there isn't one."

"If you've got a better suggestion, Sinister, I'm all ears."

John said nothing. Swapping his empty saucepan for a very full chamber pot, he tipped its grimy contents over the side.

It may have been slow going, but it worked. Bit by bit the bilge began to empty. "Must be all that fine caulking we did," said John, as he helped Jacko and Mr Jones out of their dark hole and back into the hold.

Jacko leant on John to take off his shoes and socks. "That or all the wood's swelled up now she's wet again, pluggin' up the gaps," he said, wringing out his socks.

"That too, I guess."

"How's she looking up top?"

"She's looked better," said John.

On deck, Jacko had them pull in the balloon, gathering it in a pile down the centre of the ship. He inspected the holes whilst the rest of them sorted out the rope lines that held the balloon in place. They had just finished putting everything somewhere out of the way when Captain Tonbo came back out on deck, flexing the fingers of her recently repaired mechanical arm as she went.

"Report, Mr Jackson."

"The ship's water tight for now captain, but there's no telling how long that'll last. I'd like to get her on dry land as soon as possible. Far as I can tell the balloon's fine, apart from the two big 'oles in her starboard side. Once we patch 'em I reckon she'll hold gas again, provided we can fill 'er up from down here. No butcher's bill to speak of, I'm glad to say. Just a lot of wet feet and hurt pride. I... I'm sorry, Captain. We failed you. We should never've let 'em get as close as they did. We messed up good and proper and no mistake. We... that is, I, take full responsibility. If'n you wants me resignation you can 'ave it, no bother."

"That will not be necessary, Mr Jackson. Someone messed up, but it was not you." The captain cast a baleful look at her husband, who was trying his best to be invisible.

"I saw they got in through the cabin window, Cap'n. Can I ask 'ow much they got, if'n that's alright?"

"Of course you can ask, Mr Jackson. It is your money too. They got it all. Every last penny we had."

"All of it!" exclaimed Mick.

"Yes. All of it."

"But they never– I mean, how can they– I mean—" Mick grasped at the air as if somehow that would help him find the right words. He slumped against the side of the ship, lost in his own head, as was everyone except John and Agnes.

"I don't get it," said Agnes. "Why is everyone surprised they took it all? Isn't that what pirates do, rob people?"

"That's true, so it is," said Mr Jones. "But they don't normally takes it all, like. Normally they leaves us a bit of something to see us through. Some travelling money, if you will, seeing as how, if'n we can't come back, they can't rob us again next time."

"Wi' nothin' to resupply wiv we ain't goin' nowhere," said Jacko. "We's quite lit'rally dead in the water, in fact."

"That will not happen," said Captain Tonbo firmly. "You see about getting the ship back to shore, and I will see about getting her back in the air. This is *not* the end for us, do you understand?"

John didn't know if she was saying that because she believed it or because she wanted it to be true, but it did the trick for Jacko right enough. Standing tall, he gave the captain the crispest of naval salutes. "Aye, Captain! Just leave it to me."

Captain Tonbo returned to her cabin, pursued by her husband.

Jacko paced up and down the deck, looking for somewhere to put his newfound sense of purpose. "Right, which of youse can swim? Coz I reckon it can't be more'n a quarter mile to shore, so the sooner one'a yous gets your 'ead wet, the sooner we can– What the hell is that?"

Out on the choppy waters, a stubby little steamboat was putt-putt-putting its way towards them, piloted by a leathery-looking man in a grubby captain's hat. It pulled alongside the ship, the boat coming to rest against the *Dragonfly's* hull with the gentlest of touches.

The boat's pilot squinted up at the crew gathered along the side. "Now then, looks like you lot could do with a tow ashore, eh?"

"We could that, aye," said Jacko.

"Right, well, toss us a rope an' we'll see what we can do about that."

"Thankee kindly, sir. Much appreciated."

The little tugboat pulled round in front of the *Dragonfly* and they secured a rope between the two ships. Taking up the slack, the tug's pilot pointed her towards the town they flew over on their way into the lake and gave it her all, the little boat towing the much larger ship to shore with relative ease.

"It never ceases to amaze me," said Agnes. "Soon as you get out of town people are always willin' to lend a hand."

"Yup. It's a different world alright," said John.

"Say, where's that cat of yours? I ain't seen him in a while."

The question took John by surprise. With everything that had gone on he'd forgotten all about Dexter. "Neither have I, now you mention it. Not since the fight at least." He scanned the deck of the ship, expecting Dexter to pop up at any moment. "I hope he's alright."

"I wouldn't worry about it," said Agnes. "Wherever he's got to, I'm sure he's fine."

Dexter awoke with a head full of grinding gears and no idea where he was. He thought there was something wrong with his gyroscope until he realised he was lying face down in a coil of rope. Twisting himself upright, he poked his head above the top of the rope to take in his unfamiliar surroundings.

He was on a boat, but it wasn't the *Dragonfly*, which unfortunately made perfect sense. He remembered following the thief aboard the pirate ship, and trying to get the money back by sinking his claws into the little man's soft fleshy bits (these meat-sacks were so squishy he was spoiled for choice). He remembered the thief squealing a lot, running about whilst steadfastly refusing to let go of any of the cash, and he definitely remembered getting hit in the head with something hard and unforgiving, but after that it was all a bit of a blur. He wasn't sure how he ended up hidden in the coil of rope, and he had no idea what time it was. For all he knew it could've been the next day.

Climbing from his hiding place, Dexter peeked over the ship's railing. Either the sky had gotten very rocky or the airship was in a big cave, although it also seemed to be over water as well, which didn't make a lot of sense. But, then again, when did anything these meat-sacks got up to ever make sense?

The pirates were all sitting round a little campfire, celebrating their successful heist with beer and whatnot (Dexter assumed), all except the thief, who was sat off to the side with his trousers around his ankles, tending to his wounds with a sad look upon his face.

Dexter chuckled. *Good,* he thought. *If he's still bleeding that means I wasn't out for long, which means the money is still here somewhere, which means I can get it back. If I can find out where it is, that is. Now, if I were a big pile of stolen cash where would I be?*

Dexter slipped off the ship via the gangplank and hid behind an empty barrel. Looking past the impromptu party, he spied a couple of tented living quarters at the back of the cave. They didn't look very comfortable, but they did look like the kind of place you'd store something illicit, so, creeping around the campfire, Dexter made his way over to begin his search.

It wasn't a big port the *Dragonfly* found herself being towed towards. Bowness-On-Windermere was a tourist town. Lots of twee houses, semi-grand hotels, and souvenir shops, all built from copious amounts of the local slate. The only ships it saw day-to-day were steam cruisers and pleasure boats. Something like the *Dragonfly* arriving was starting to draw a crowd already, despite how early it was, and at the head of that crowd stood the policeman, John Kent.

"Looks like you folks've been through the wars," he said, as the crew disembarked their battered ship.

"We have indeed," replied Captain Tonbo.

"Is everyone alright? Do you need a doctor at all?"

"No, we are fine. Thank you."

"Good. I'm glad to hear it." Constable Kent pointed to a pub at the other end of the jetty. "I've asked Auld Bill to open The Kettle early so you folks can have a rest and a cuppa. I imagine you could do with one after what you've been through."

Captain Tonbo offered Constable Kent a short bow of gratitude. "Thank you, officer. That is most kind."

Constable Kent bobbed his head in return. "Not at all, ma'am. My pleasure." He looked up at the darkening sky. "Actually, I might join you, if that's alright? Looks like things are about to get a bit wet out here." He considered the pools of water squidging out of the shoes of a lot of the crew. "Or should that be 'wetter'?"

As the crew headed for the pub, John pulled Agnes to one side. "Tie your jacket around your waist," he said.

"What? Why?"

"Well, you ripped your pants during the fight," said John. "And, um..." He pointed down and around the back, unwilling to finish that sentence. Agnes felt around behind herself and her eyes widened.

"Good looking out, Sinister," she said, tying her jacket around her waist. "Although what were you doing looking there in the first place, hmm?"

"I, um– That is to say—"

Agnes grinned as John turned bright red and scuttled off. Then she frowned as the first drops of rain landed on her head.

Dexter found nothing of interest in the living quarters, and not much in the storage area next to them. Just a lot of dust and empty shelves. There were a few boxes left to stick his nose into but he was already certain that the cash was in someone's pocket, and if so it was going to be very hard to get back. That thief may have been as soft as a ripe banana, but the rest of this lot looked hard as nails and twice as pointy.

He snuck closer to the camp to hear what they were talking about.

"I don't get it, if you wanna break with Fenris then why give him his cut?"

"Coz I want to see the look on his face when I tell him where he can shove it, that's why."

"He won't like it."

"He's not meant to like it."

"I mean he might start, is what I'm tryin' to say."

"Which is why we're taking the lads with us, innit."

She must be the one with the money, thought Dexter. *The one pacing up and down with the murderous look in her eye. Now, how to get it out of her pocket and into mine?*

He watched as the gang got their things together – their 'things' being half a dozen knives and a pickaxe shaft each – trying to decide what his next move should be. He saw the woman go over to a large lockbox by the fire that one of the gang had been sitting on. She pulled a thick sheaf of notes from her inside jacket pocket, stuffed a few back where they came from, and deposited the rest in the lockbox, using an ornate iron key to lock it with a resounding *thunk*. She handed the box to the little thief, who thankfully now had his trousers back on.

"Stay here, hang on to this, and keep an eye on Sue. We won't be long." The thief nodded, relieved not to be part of the upcoming fight.

That does it, thought Dexter, as he watched the thief totter off with the very heavy box. *I'm never getting that out of here, not by myself. I'm gonna need that key.*

Dexter followed the woman towards the front of the cave, where the rest of the gang was waiting by the narrow path that led to the outside world. It was raining outside, the sort of heavy rain people like to describe as being like cats and dogs for some reason (Dexter had never gotten his head around that). He hoped the rain would be enough to make them change their mind but nope, off they went, and the key with them, right out into the wet like it was nothing at all.

Well that's lovely, that is, thought Dexter, giving the wall of water a baleful look. *Could this day get any worse?* He hesitated at the cave mouth. He wasn't bothered about getting wet, not in any technical sense – he was, for all intents and purposes, waterproof – he just didn't see the need to do it deliberately, not if he had any other choice. The thing is, he didn't see that he had any other choice.

Dexter trotted out into the rain. A bolt of lightning ripped across the sky. Dexter ran back into the cave again. He might be waterproof, but he was still made of metal, and according to his maker, Nomko, metal and lightning did not go together. He might be fine, he might get away with being on an exposed mountainside in the pouring rain during a horrendous thunder storm, but why risk it if he didn't have to? *Especially* for somebody else's money. He liked the crew of the *Dragonfly* (as much as he liked any other bunch of meat-sacks) just not enough to fry his analysis engine for.

Dexter stood at the cave mouth having a good shiver. He'd only been outside for two seconds, yet he was soaked through. How did that happen?

He turned to head back into the cave only to find a little girl standing in his path, a strange look upon her rather serious face. *Where the hell did she come from?* he wondered, glancing left and right for a non-existent way out. "Meow?" he said unconvincingly, tilting his head in that way people seemed to like so much. The little girl's frown grew even deeper.

Producing a dirty piece of cloth from behind her back, she advance on Dexter's trapped, shivering form with great intent.

The Steaming Kettle was a cosy little pub, the kind where people kept their own tankard on a hook behind the bar, decorated with polished horse brasses and pictures of local landmarks that all started to look the same after a while. Its owner, Auld Bill, had lit a fire and was handing round sandwiches and mugs of tea as though all his Christmases had come at once. On a day like today, he'd have been lucky to get maybe two of his most enthusiastic locals in, nursing their drinks for hours on end whilst they put the world to rights. Having a whole crew in willing to eat and drink whatever you put in front of them was a gift from God, and he intended to make the most of it before the rains stopped and they all cleared off again.

John glanced out the pub's front window looking for the *Dragonfly*, but all he saw out there was a good reason to stay indoors. He didn't envy Jacko and Mick, who had gone to batten down the airship's hatches (whatever that meant). They must be getting soaked through.

A sausage roll appeared in front of John. He tucked in without a second thought, dipping it between bites into the small pot of Parliament Sauce that had come with it. On the other side of the table, Agnes was doing battle with a Cornish pastie wider than John's head, washing it down with a whole pot of tea, whilst beside her Constable Kent seemed happy with just a cup of tea and a slice of cake (although he hadn't been in a fight for his life a few hours earlier. That kind of thing will give you quite an appetite).

"Does it rain this bad all the time?" John asked the constable, nodding towards the window.

"I'd like to say no, but this is pretty normal for this time of year," the constable replied.

"I dunno how you can stand it."

The constable shrugged. "Without the rain, there'd be no lakes."

Fair enough, thought John, finishing off his sausage roll.

The constable played with the lip of his mug, twisting it on the table in a distracted manner. "So you say these pirates cleaned you out, took everything they could. That's... unusual."

"So everyone keeps saying," said John.

"Any idea why they would do that?" asked Agnes. "Seeing as, as you say, it's so unusual."

"Not really, no. Although that's not the part that worries me."

"What is?"

"The fact that one lot fired on the other. That is a most unwelcome development." John and Agnes exchanged a look of confusion. "The clan on the ground, shooting their harpoons at the one in the air," explained Constable Kent. "That's a proper no-no around here. That's crossing the line in no uncertain terms. Any clan willing to do that is willing to go to war, and that is not something any of us should be taking lightly."

"Do you think it has anything to do with that airship going down? A shift in the balance of power between the four clans, as it were," said John.

Constable Kent seemed surprised at John's understanding of the situation. He looked at Agnes who dismissed his concerns with a wave of the hand. "John's the partner I told you about the other night. What I know, he knows."

Constable Kent didn't seem to like the situation, but he at least appeared willing to accept it. "Yes, that is exactly what I think. And if that is indeed the case then things may be about to get very messy around here indeed. As I explained to Miss Dexter, the reiver clans are a part of everybody's lives, even my own. If people have to take sides they will, and they won't be shy about it neither."

"Shame you don't know where they are. You could go ask them what's going on," said John.

"Oh, I know where they are," said Constable Kent. "Everybody does." John nearly choked on his drink.

"What? You know where they are? Then why don't you go arrest them or something? That's you job, innit?" The constable burst out laughing. "What? What did I say?"

Constable Kent pointed across the room. "You see Auld Jack there, behind the bar. The one rushing about with all the tea and biscuits. Do you think he'd be so forthcoming if he thought I was making any serious effort to interfere with the clans at all? His nephew's part of the Long Souths, and his neighbour's boy does some work with the Defenders of the March. They all come in here when they're in town, putting their ill-gotten gains right in Auld Jack's pocket. I told you, the reiver clans are a part of the Lake District. In many ways they *are* the Lake District. If I started arresting them, I'd end up arresting everybody, and I haven't got the time." Constable Kent considered John thoughtfully. "You on the other hand are free to do whatever you like."

"Me! I'm not going to arrest nobody. Are you mad?!"

"No, not arrest. But talk to, maybe, see if you can find out what's going on. I could tell you where to find the Western Riders, the ones with the airship. You could go and see why they decided to clean you out instead of taking their usual cut. And while you're there maybe you could see what's going on between them and the Long Souths, see if there's a feud brewing or something. That'd be valuable information to a man like me. We could maybe see our way to lining your pocket for such information, if the local magistrate approves, that is."

"He can approve all he likes, I ain't doin' it. What's to stop 'em chopping me 'ead off soon as look at me?"

"They wouldn't do that. The Riders are a reasonable bunch. They'd just tell you to eff off and send you on your way probably. There's nothing to worry about."

"I ain't worried coz I ain't doin' it. You go and talk to 'em if it's as easy as all that."

"I can't, I told you. It's not for me to get involved, not if I wants to keep doing what I do."

"Well you can forget about me doing anything like that. I'm not that stupid."

"You were all for having a nice cosy chat with 'em last night," said Agnes.

"That was before one of 'em tried to stick a sword in me. I think it's safe to say that I have reconsidered my position since then."

Hearing raised voices, Captain Tonbo came over. She had been talking with Mr Jones, but now it seemed that the chef had decided to have a nap. He lay curled up on a bench at the back of the bar, a borrowed blanket over his head. Going full berserker can really take it out of you. "Is everything alright?" she asked, pushing aside the plate of sandwiches that magically arrived at the same time she did.

"Everything's fine, Captain," said Agnes. "Constable Kent here was trying to persuade John to go see the pirates who attacked us, see if he can't get your money back for you."

"Really? That does not sound very likely."

"No, it's not," said John. "Thank you, Captain. I'm glad someone round here can see sense."

"I meant the part about getting the money back." The captain turned to Constable Kent. "You can really make that happen? Mr Sinister and the pirates in the same room together."

Constable Kent nodded. "I can, yes."

"No, he can't."

"Then we should give it a try, should we not?"

"No, we should not," John insisted. "Look, I appreciate everyone's enthusiasm to risk my neck on some wild goose chase, but you can forget it." He jabbed a finger in turn at Constable Kent and Captain Tonbo. "I don't work for you, *or* for you – despite recent events – so no matter what anyone says I ain't gonna do it. No way, no how, no chance, forget it. Find some other idiot for this hair-brained scheme of yours, coz this idiot is staying right here!"

The door to the pub opened and in stumbled Jacko and Mick. They stood by the door, shaking out their jackets with one hand as they fended off Auld Jack's cheese rolls with the other.

"Is the ship secure, Mr Jackson?"

"She is that, Captain. She is that." Jacko stomped over to the fire.

"And what about my cat?" asked John. "Did you see him when you were, um, battenberging things up?"

"I didn't, no. What about you, Mick?"

"What's that? The cat? I've not seen him since the fight."

John shot to his feet. "Wait, you saw him during the fight! When? How?"

"Right before we cut away, on the pirate ship. He had one of the pirates by the short and curlies. Why, what's going on?"

"His cat's missing," said Agnes.

"Did you see him get off?" said John. "Was he back on board the *Dragonfly* before she went down?"

"Beats me," said Mick. "But I doubt it. I don't think he would have had the time."

John sank back into his chair. "So he probably went off with the pirates."

"Probably," said Mick, still unsure what was going on.

At the table, Agnes watched John wrestle with his own conscience. "It's just a cat, y'know. You don't have to do it."

"Yes I do," said John. "It's complicated. He's… he's not your average cat, y'know?" Agnes nodded, as if she did indeed know.

"What's going on?" said Constable Kent. "What's this about a cat?"

John rubbed his face. He was regretting taking on this job. "How do I get to these pirates, then? I assume there's some sort of hideout or something?"

"There is. Not too far from here actually."

"Can you show me? It seems I need to go see a man about a cat."

"A woman about a cat. The leader of the Western Riders is a woman. And no, I can't. If they see me coming they might shoot first and ask questions later. But I know a man who can." Constable Kent pushed himself to standing. "Sit tight. I'll be back in a bit with your guide. Have another sarnie while I'm gone. From what I hear, the salted pork is particularly good."

Pushing his way out into the rain, the constable disappeared within yards of leaving the pub. John shivered at the thought of walking out into such nonsense. "I hope Dexter's alright. I can't imagine what it'd be like for him in the middle of all that lot."

"I'm sure he's fine," said Agnes, checking the contents of a nearby roll. "You know what they say, cat's always land on their feet."

Cats maybe, thought John. *But what about cat-shaped automatons? What do they land on?*

It turned out the mechanical cat had indeed landed on his feet. The dour little girl he'd encountered in the cave mouth had dried him off, given him some bread to eat (Dexter would have preferred some of the kindling by the fire, easier for his boiler to handle, but even a little girl might view a cat eating twigs and dried leaves as a bit suspicious), and now she sat watching over him whilst he lapped up water from a chipped ceramic bowl.

She was a quiet one, this little girl. Not like Sinister's niece, who yammered away ten to the dozen whenever Dexter was around. She had this look on her face like she was busy trying to figure out the world (or, quite possibly, like she had already figured it out and was unimpressed by what she saw). So far she had been nice, but Dexter was keeping his eye on her. These meat-sacks could turn on you at a moment's notice, even the little ones. *Especially* the little ones, in fact. Quite often you didn't know someone was a cat kicker until there was a pair of size twelves swinging at your head; and by then, of course, it was too late. So he kept his distance, which thankfully was easy enough to do, since the little girl seemed determined to do the same.

Over by the fire, the thief, who had fallen asleep with his feet on the lockbox, awoke with a start. He stretched and looked around – Dexter was hidden from sight behind some crates – scratching idly at himself as he searched the ground for something. Tossing a couple of logs on the fire, he shifted a small black cooking pot into the centre of the increasing flame.

The thief called out to the little girl. "Hey, Sue, I'm heating up some stew. Do you want some?" Sat with her back to the fire, the little girl ignored him. "I said, do you– Oh, right."

The little girl saw the change in light and pulled a blanket down over Dexter just as the thief came round to stand in front of her. He waved, even though she was already looking right at him. "Do, you, want, some, food?" he said very deliberately, pointing at the little girl and miming eating. The little girl wagged her finger, frowning. "Erm, right, I know this. That means 'what', right?" The thief wagged his finger back at her and the little girl nodded. "I don't know what the sign for stew is. Um, let's see..." The thief made bunny ears with his fingers and hopped his hand around. The little girl didn't laugh. She rubbed her closed fist in a circle on her stomach, shaking her head. The thief panicked until the little girl simply shook her head, placing the fingers of a flat hand on her chin and pulling them away; *No thank you*. In a moment of triumph, the thief remembered the sign for, *You're welcome*, a beckoning gesture using both hands that always seemed like offering someone out to him. The little girl half smiled at his awkward movements and the thief smiled back, happy that he had made an effort and for once it hadn't been a complete disaster.

Dexter looked up at the little girl, Sue, whose head was turned to keep an eye on the retreating thief. "Are you deaf?" he asked, which he knew was a stupid thing to say to a potentially deaf person but he couldn't think of anything else to say. "Sue. Hey, Sue." The little girl looked down at Dexter. Had she heard him? Had he just outed himself to a meat-sack other than Sinister? If he had she didn't seem all that bothered about it. Either talking cats were ten a penny round here or she hadn't heard him at all.

Dexter felt like an ass for doing it but he had to know for sure. He turned his head, covering his mouth with his paw like he had an itch to scratch. "Can you hear me?" he mumbled. He looked back but the little girl was too busy fishing an apple out of her pocket to pay him any attention. Polishing it with the palm of her grubby hand, she took a bite, juice running down her chin. She spotted Dexter looking and offered him a bite too, but the cat simply shook his head.

"Nah, I'm good," he said, pushing the apple back towards her with his paw.

Only when the little girl frowned at him did Dexter realise what he'd done.

Molly Sigurdsson kicked open the door to the Striding Edge and marched inside. Soaking wet and covered in mud, she surveyed the room whilst the rest of her crew stumbled in behind her. It had been a hard slog up the mountain, in the midst of all that wind and rain, but none of them had dared complain. They knew when their boss was in a killing mood, and they knew better than to put themselves on the receiving end of it for the sake of some damp socks and a river of cold water running down the back of your neck.

The inn was, unsurprisingly, almost empty. Just the one shepherd over by the fire – his stocking feet up on the grate, staring into the bottom of his glass with the grim determination of someone who can see trouble coming and wants no part of it – and Fenris Wolf behind the bar, polishing glasses with a smile on his face like he hadn't a care in the world.

Toby came through from the back carrying three bowls of a stew he'd just finished making on a tray. It was Mrs Mulligan's night off so he was on kitchen duty. He'd made a rather nice leek and potato, with added tarragon to give it that extra something special. He wasn't sure if it worked or not, but he liked it.

Catching sight of Molly and her crew, Toby turned pale and dropped the tray, the delicious stew hitting the floor with a sloppy, well-seasoned crash.

"Damn it, boy. Watch what you're doing," barked Fenris. "Fetch a cloth an' wipe that up afore it stains."

"Stay there, Toby," said Molly.

Eyes wide, Toby froze on the spot, unsure whether going or staying was least likely to get him killed.

Fenris appeared to notice Molly for the first time. "Molly! Lads. What are you doing out on a day like this?"

Stepping forward, Molly reached into her jacket pocket. "I've come to settle up."

"Well that's very good of you, but you didn't have to do that. Tomorrow would have done fi—" Molly flung a handful of notes in Fenris's face. The paper money exploded around his head, fluttering to the ground in the silence of a whole room holding its breath. Fenris picked up a note that had landed on his shoulder and placed it gently on the bar. "Is something wrong, Molly?"

"Don't come the innocent with me, Fenris. You knew, didn't you?!"

"Knew? Knew what?"

"What Little Neck was planning." Fenris looked suitably confused. "Attacking us the next time we went out. You probably put him up to it, in fact."

"Oh! Yes, I heard about Little Neck trying to take your score. Shocking that. Truly shocking. But I assure you, I had nothing to do with it. How could I? I'm not in charge of the Long Souths."

"Oh come on. Everyone knows Little Neck wouldn't do something like that without your permission. I *saw* him, in here, talking with your boy, Toby." Molly jabbed a finger in Toby's direction and he flinched. "And he weren't after no score neither. He wanted to sink us. You know how I *know* he wasn't after the money?" Molly leant on the bar, bringing herself and Fenris within reach of each other. "There was no line in his harpoon, Fenris. He wasn't tryin' to hook us an' reel us in. He wanted to put us down, one way or a bloody n'other."

A look flickered across Fenris's face. Was it surprise? Confusion? General annoyance. Whatever it was, he soon got ahold of himself.

"Molly, whatever happened between you and the Long Souths has got nothing to do with me. But you do make a good point. If I *were* in charge I could make sure stuff like this never happens again. It's because we're all at each other's throats all the time that stuff like this happens. But if we worked together, with me offering guidance to all the clans' leaders, there's no reason why we all couldn't prosper."

Molly burst out laughing.

"Wow. Just... wow. You are unbelievable." Molly stepped right up to the bar, looking Fenris dead in the eye. "I will never follow you, Fenris. Never. You know why? Because you are a fool. Which is fine, some of my best friends are fools, but you are the worst kind of fool, because you have no idea how foolish you actually are. You think you're smart because you bully and threaten people into doing your bidding, then when things work out you act like the success is all because of you, when in fact it's because of the people around you not letting the world come apart. And when they *can't* stop you from making a big mess of things you blame them, saying 'If only they'd done what I'd told them to do, everything would have worked out fine.' Because that's how stupid you are, Fenris. You think the sun shines out of your own backside, and that the rest of us should be thankful for being allowed to bask in its rancid glory. Well I'm here to tell you that there's only one thing coming out the back end of you. It stinks, it's unpleasant, and it's only slightly more worthless than the stuff that comes out of your mouth.

"Unfortunately, you seem to have an endless supply of both, so I'm done. That's it for me. I ain't never coming back here again." She waved her hand at the money on the bar. "That there is the last you're getting outta the Western Riders. From now on you're on your own."

Molly turned and headed for the door.

Fenris reached under the bar and laid his hand on something sharp and dangerous. He caught sight of Magnus Sigurdsson watching him, crossbow in hand. Extracting his hand slowly, he placed a pound note that had landed in one of the drip trays on the bar next to the rest of the money. "This isn't enough," he said. "I heard you scored big this time. I wants me proper cut."

"So sue me," Molly called over her shoulder. "You know where I am." She paused by the front door. "Oh, and, Toby, please inform your father that I would marry one of his donkeys before I would ever consider marrying anything that came from his pox-ridden loins. There's a good lad."

Molly left, her crew walking out backwards after her. Behind the bar, Fenris Wolf crushed the handful of notes in his fist, an enraged snarl spreading across his already angry face.

Toby, his boots covered in lumps of congealed stew, turned to his father. "Marry? What does she mean marry? Who's getting married?"

Toby ran from the room as something sharp and dangerous was thrown at his head.

It must have been late afternoon by the time Constable Kent returned to the Steaming Kettle, but it was hard to tell. John's watch had stopped working, and the unchanging grey light that filtered in through the front window gave little clue as to the time of day. He was keeping track by the food Auld Jack kept producing from the pub's kitchen. They'd just had scones, and he could smell someone working on a roast back there, so he reckoned it was somewhere between four and five, give or take a ginger snap or two.

The constable had brought with him a skinny young man with wild hair and a ready smile who John recognised from the Striding Edge a couple of nights ago; the one playing Happy Families with the little girl. He had on the same mismatched tweeds as before and, like the constable, he was pretty much soaked to the bone.

Constable Kent brought the young man over to John and Agnes's table. They were sitting alone, the rest of the crew having retreated to the back of the pub to drown their sorrows in silence. "Miss Dexter, Mr Sinister, I'd like to introduce you to Billy, the best guide this side of the Pennines."

John shook Billy's hand. "Pleased to meet you, Billy. Have a seat."

The young man beamed as he shook hands all round. "Likewise, I'm sure. The constable said you folks were in need of a guide?"

John, catching wind of the young man's wet tweeds, shuffled a little further away from him. "We are. You're familiar with the reiver clans, I take it."

The young man's smile became very fixed. "I am."

"Well we need to speak with some of them, and we've been told you can help us with that."

The young man looked to Constable Kent, but the constable seemed more interested in the sticky bun he had discovered. "Are you sure that is such a good idea? The clans are not very, um, enthusiastic about meeting new people."

John sighed. "No. It's a terrible idea. But unfortunately we don't seem to have much choice in the matter. Can you take us to them or not?"

The young man glanced again at Constable Kent, whose interest in the sticky bun made it quite clear that whatever was about to be said was not going to be heard by him. "That all depends on who it is you want to meet," he said. "Some of them are a little friendlier than others. Or a little less murdery, should I say."

"Apparently we need to talk to the West Riders," said John.

"The Western Riders," corrected Constable Kent.

"Right. Yeah. Them lot."

"Oh really!" said the young man, his enthusiasm going up a notch. "And, er, what is it you want to talk to them about, if I may? Is it something they're going to… like?"

John mulled the question over as he took a sip of lukewarm tea. "Let's just say it's not something that'll annoy them too much."

"Fingers crossed," said Agnes.

"Yes, thank you, Agnes," said John. "So what do you say? Can you take us to them or not?"

"Us?" said the young man. "So, the both of you then?" He looked at Agnes, imagining her arriving unannounced on someone's front doorstep. Agnes shook her head, smiling.

"Nope. Just him. I'm staying here where it's nice and warm."

"Oh. Oh, right. I see. Yes, well, in that case, I can do that for you. No problem. But not today."

"What? Why not today?" said John.

Billy pointed out the window like the answer was obvious. "Tonight will be a stormy night, you to the town must go," he said rather grandly. John frowned. Billy shrugged. "It's easy enough to get lost around here, never mind with all that lot going on. Even if we made it to the Riders we might not make it back again. We're not going anywhere 'til this lets up, and that isn't going to happen 'til tomorrow. Trust me, I know."

John looked to Constable Kent, who nodded his confirmation.

"Right. So we set off in the morning then. What time can you be here?"

"Oh, I'll stay the night. No way I'm walking home in this. Seriously, you think this is bad, wait until you see it an hour from now. You wouldn't wish it on your worst enemy."

One thing Dexter liked about being a cat, which these meat-sacks would never understand, was the joy of a good perch. Finding just the right spot to sit and watch the world go by, putting yourself above and beyond whatever craziness was going on down below, was a gift beyond measure.

By the time the pirate gang returned, Dexter made sure he'd found himself a nice little stone shelf in the wall of the cave from which to observe their comings and goings. He didn't want them knowing he was there until it became unavoidable. There was no telling what they might do, and in his experience cat kickers came in all shapes and sizes. It wasn't the most comfortable perch he'd ever been on, but it was out of the way and he could see everything going on around him, so he would put up with it for now.

The gang didn't seem too happy with whatever had transpired out there in the rain, which came as no surprise to Dexter. What had started out as a bit of bracing dampness in the air had turned into a wall of water which you could easily swim through, if you were so inclined. Nothing good could come of a night like this.

"Hopefully that's the last we'll see of Fenris Wolf and his lot for a while," the woman who appeared to be in charge declared.

"You know it isn't," one of the men said, a young guy about her age with a big crossbow. "He'll probably come after us now, y'know, especially the way you talked to him in front of everyone."

The woman didn't like that. She charged at the man in a rage. "You think I should have been nicer, do you? Kissed his arse a bit. Said please and thank you after what he did to us!"

The young man held his ground. "No, I'm just sayin', I don't see Fenris walking away from this, not without getting a few digs in first."

The woman, to her credit, knew good advice when she heard it. "Yeah, I know. We need to be on our guard for a while, in case he tries something. The Long Souths too. I wouldn't put it past Little Neck to chance his arm, given what's gone on already."

"What about Shapside Stan? Do you think he'd try owt?"

"I doubt it. Stan's not going to do Fenris any favours, not on purpose anyhow. He might be up for sticking it to the Long Souths though, given everything that's gone on between them. We should get a message to him, let him know what's what."

The young man didn't seem to like that idea. "Are you looking to start a war?"

"I ain't lookin', no. But if there's one comin' I'll be more than happy to oblige."

Dexter didn't know who all these people were, these Long Souths and Little Necks and Fenris bloody Wolfs, but he got the distinct impression a lot of them would be dead by the end of the week.

The meat-sack looking to start a war seemed to realise that they had an audience, the rest of the gang trying to pretend they couldn't hear what was going on in the rather small, rather echoey cave. "Set a watch and make sure we stay safe until morning," she said softly. "We can talk some more about this then."

"I hope so," said the man. "Coz we need to figure out how we're going to make money now the Striding Edge is out of bounds."

The woman didn't seem to have an answer for that, but it was clear it was something that concerned her too. The man went off to see to the crew, whilst the woman went looking for the little girl, Sue.

She found her doing what she always did, keeping out the way of the grownups.

Dexter watched the two of them communicate in that flappy hand language he'd seen the thief try and use. It was the most animated he'd seen the little girl since he'd got there (which admittedly was only fairly recently).

It must he hard, he thought, not being able to talk to people. Sure, you had the hand thing, but if the other person didn't know that, or wasn't very good at it, what then? Probably something similar to the way he'd had to be for the first year of his life. He'd only been allowed to talk to a few people, keeping his real nature secret to see if he could pass for a real cat. That had been pretty boring, so he'd had to amuse himself when those two weren't around. Mostly that involved napping and chasing mice, both with varying degrees of success, but a lot of the time it meant coming up with little games and such to distract yourself from the truth, that you'd give anything for someone to talk to if only for a little while. Things had gotten better since Sinister had arrived on the scene, but it was still hard.

All he wanted was to be the same as everyone else, to laugh and joke and complain about things all the time, but that was never going to happen. Even if your average meat-sack could deal with the idea of a talking cat, he'd never be the same as them. He'd always be different, separate, part of The Other, and there was nothing he could do to change that.

Dexter saw the woman kiss the girl on the forehead and walk away. Hopping down from his rocky perch, he went over to where the little girl was sitting.

Despite his slip up earlier, she didn't seem to suspect he wasn't a real cat. It was time to make the most of that. Rubbing his head against the girl's hand, Dexter started purring, burying his face in her palm so that she would feel the vibrations. When he felt her start to stroke his head, he climbed into her lap, looking up at her the way he did when he wanted Sinister's niece, Emily, to bring him a treat. Sue didn't coo and melt the way Emily did, but she did wrap her arms around him, bending forward so she could bury her face in his fur.

They stayed like that until it was time for Sue to go to bed, Dexter finding a spot next to her on the pile of blankets she slept on so that he would be the first thing she saw when she awoke the next day.

The rain beat down on the deck of the *Dragonfly* like a landslide of rock on a giant coffin lid. It was not conducive to a good night's sleep, which was why John and Agnes were sitting in the hold, discussing what their next move should be.

Billy the guide was there too, but he kept himself to himself, more interested in scribbling things down in his notebook than he was in their conversation.

"The captain thinks you might get some of her money back, y'know," said Agnes.

John sighed. "I know. As if there wasn't enough riding on this already."

"Do you think you might? Get some of the cash back, I mean."

"Of course not. Can you see that lot giving anything up without a fight? Coz I can't."

Agnes watched John. "You don't have to go, y'know, not if you think it's a bad idea."

"I do though, don't I?"

"I guess so," said Agnes, not entirely convinced. They sat for a moment listening to the rain. "And you're sure you don't want me there with you tomorrow?"

"No. I mean, yes, of course I do, but best not. It doesn't sound like it'd go down too well."

"Yeah, I guess not."

Pressing her back against the side of the ship, Agnes lifted her hips and pulled at the seat of her pants. Since she'd ripped her weekday suit she'd had no choice but to don her best bouncer's uniform, a very stylish, very fitting set of clothes that were not made for sitting on the ground.

"You can head back tomorrow if you like," said John. "You don't need to be here anymore."

"You sure about that?"

"Yeah. If I can't get answers out of this lot there's not much else I can do. I'll probably head back myself, if I make it out in one piece."

"Well thanks, but if it's all the same to you I'll stick around an' see what happens. I mean, let's be honest, what you think'll happen and what actually does happen are often two very different things."

John smiled. "Thanks, Agnes. I was hoping you'd say that."

Jacko came into the hold with a cloth bundle under his arm. He dropped it at Agnes's feet.

Agnes frowned. "What's this? I ain't doin' no more work, y'know. That bit's done with now."

"I made yer these," said Jacko. Agnes unfolded the bundle to reveal a pair of white cotton trousers with a thick blue ribbon down the side, and a loose cotton shirt complete with triangular blue collar that tied at the front and more blue ribbon at the cuff. "They're nowt special, but they'll last a sight longer than them fancy-schmancy pants of yours. And they won't rip first sign of trouble neither. Thanks fer not gettin' us killed afore, with the harpoon and that. That were... Well, you done alright. Alright?"

Agnes took in the exquisite stitching around the waist and down the trouser leg. Not only would they last a long time, they looked like they might actually fit too. "I—" started Agnes, but when she looked up Jacko was already on his way out the door. "Thank you!" she called after him. Jacko paused at the door to give her a quick nod before disappearing from sight.

"Well," said John. "I didn't see that coming."

Agnes climbed to her feet. "I'm gonna try them on." She left the hold, leaving John alone with the still scribbling Billy.

John went over to where he sat next to a candle and a pot of ink. "What's that you're doing?"

Billy half closed his notebook, feigning disinterest. "Oh, y'know, this and that. Poems, stories, that kind of thing. There's not much to do round here once the sun goes down, so I write to pass the time."

"You should find yourself a wife, mate. She'd give you something to do, I'm sure."

"Oh yes? A perfect woman, nobly planned, to warm, to comfort, and command?"

"Er, something like that, mate. Yeah."

A gamut of unhappy emotion ran across Billy's face. "Yes, well, I would, but easier said than done, eh."

"Ain't that the truth," said John. He sat down next to Billy. "So, you make a good living showing people about the place?"

Billy shrugged unhappily. "Not as good as I would like, no. Most of the tourists we get up this way are only interested in tea shops and pleasure cruises. They wouldn't know a decent bit of exercise if it whacked them in the head with a pair of muddy walking boots."

John chuckled. "That's a shame. There's some decent views round here, I'll bet. When it's not raining, that is."

Billy suddenly became energised, clearly about to wax lyrical on one of his favourite topics. "Oh there are," he said. "Views like you wouldn't believe. And they're not that hard to get to either. An hour's walk from here I could show you things that would take your breath away. We wouldn't even have to go that high. Mountains, and lakes, and fell-side tarns, and that's just the easy stuff. For those willing to put in the effort, well, you've been up to Striding Edge, you know how gorgeous it is round there."

"I hear you," said John, trying to back away from the subject before the man really got going. "Shame there's not more interest in that kind of thing."

"Oh, there'd be plenty of interest if they knew what was out there, believe me there would," said Billy, brandishing his notebook like it was the key to everything. "All we've got to do is get the word out and folk'll come running, you mark my words."

"I'm sure they will," said John, fairly sure that they wouldn't. Who was going to hike up a hill in the rain when they could sit by the sea eating cake until the pubs were open? What kind of a holiday would that be? But he knew better than to express that to young Billy. He didn't need to spend the rest of the night being persuaded of the error of his ways.

Agnes returned to the hold in her new outfit, a huge smile upon her face. "Check it out. How great is this?"

"Looks good," said John.

"Fits me like a glove an' all," said Agnes, twisting her arms and legs in all directions. "Honest to God, they're so damn comfy I might not wear anything else ever again."

"And they suit you too, miss, if I may be so bold," said Billy.

"Absolutely you may," said Agnes, squatting to check how tight the trousers were down below. "I'm telling you, that man might be a pain in the backside, but he sure knows his way around a needle and thread."

Toby once saw his friend's dog fall in the water at the top of Aira Force. He'd watched in horror as the terrified animal had tumbled over the edge of the waterfall, bouncing off every rock it could as it rushed to its inevitable death. By the time it crawled out of the river a hundred yards downstream, beaten, bloody, and barely alive, the poor thing had looked like it just wanted to lay down and die, and as he stumbled in through the front door of The Striding Edge, finally free of the storm that raged outside, Toby Wolf could certainly understand why.

Four men came in after him, four big men, with big hands, big swords, and big scowls on their miserable, ugly faces. They barged past Toby and stomped over to the fireplace, attempting to warm themselves as they dripped all over the floor. Luckily for them, and the locals, there was no one around to complain. Fenris had closed early because of the bad weather (and certainly not because he was in a stroppy mood after the way Molly Sigurdsson had talked to him).

Toby approached the bar, where his father sat watching the measly group of men he had managed to scrounge up with a sour look upon his face.

"That's it?" said Fenris. "That's all you could find?"

It wasn't, but Toby knew better than to tell the truth. "Yes, boss."

"What about Yorkshire Bob and what's his name, that boy of his?"

"Away at a weddin'."

"Whose wedding?"

"Little Pete's."

"Who's Little Pete?"

"Bob's boy."

Fenris snorted. "And what about Big Stanley and the Thompson Boys? Where are they at?"

Well, Father, they told me to tell you in no uncertain terms where you could shove your summons on a night like this. "Oh, um, they're away too. At the wedding, like. It's a bit of a do, by all accounts."

"Really? Funny how I never got an invite."

Toby said nothing, because nothing he could say would help. He'd have to apologise to Yorkshire Bob for dropping him in it of course, but rather an awkward conversation tomorrow than a hand around your throat today.

"I guess it'll have to do," said Fenris. "Get yourself behind that bar and pour the lads some drinks. Make 'em strong and don't be stingy. We're gonna need 'em well-oiled if they're gonna go for this one, especially Lazy Larry and the Tup Worrier."

Toby did what he was told, glad to be out of the way.

"Gentlemen," said Fenris, walking over to the fire. "Thank you for coming. I appreciate it very much."

"Aye, well. The boss sez come, you come," said Lazy Larry. "Even if it is chucking it down in the middle of the night," he added under his breath. The other three grunted their agreement to both parts of what he had said (Lazy Larry was not known for his subtlety).

Fenris tried not to punch him in the face. "I have a proposition for you all, one that would see the Wolves take their rightful place among the clans of the Western March."

Lazy Larry pulled off his boots so he could dangle his wet feet close to the open fire. "I 'ope it's not more money you're after for another airship. We barely got our cash back before this one went an' crashed it into t' ground, eh." He jerked his thumb at Toby who had just arrived with a tray of drinks. They each took one, not even bothering to look Toby in the eye, let alone say thank you.

"We made a tidy profit out of the *Dauntless* before she went down," said Fenris. "More than we made out of robbin' people on the ground, that's for sure."

"So it *is* more money you're after," said Larry. "Well I hate to tell you, guv, but I'm tapped out. Me missus is doin' up the spare room an' it's costin' me an arm and leg. Don't ask me why we need a new bed in there, no one ever comes to visit, but apparently we do. An' don't get me started on curtains neither."

Lazy Larry started pulling on his boots like he was getting ready to leave, the other three making short work of their drinks as though they intended to join him. Fenris seethed as he imagined throttling Larry with his bare hands. One of the things he hated about being clan chief was the constant need for negotiation. Everyone thought the lads just did what they were told, that all he had to do was snap his fingers and they'd come running, but nothing could be further from the truth. Reivers kept their own council first, their chief's second, and generally their wife's third, and that's if you were lucky. Some of them weren't even allowed out the house these days without their wife's permission, never mind going on a raid, and here he was negotiating with these milk-sops like they were somehow his equals. It was humiliating. And it only went to prove to Fenris that he'd been right all along; marriage made a man weak, and anyone who tried to tell you otherwise was either married, female, or a combination of the two.

"It's not your money I'm after, but you're right, this is about an airship. The *Molly's Kiss* to be precise." That got their attention. "I think it's about time the Western Riders gave her up, for the greater good of all concerned. And if they're unwilling to give her up, well..."

"You want go to war with the Western Riders?"

"Not at all. No one wants a war. I just want to borrow their airship for a little while, that's all."

"How long's a little while?"

Fenris shrugged. "Forever."

The four men shifted in their seats, glancing at one another. "Ya cannae nick Magnus's ship," said Young Billy Bracewell, the eldest of the group. "There'd be hell ta pay."

"Magnus gave up the *Kiss* when he buggered off to Iceland, or wherever the hell he went. It's not his ship anymore. And besides, we don't have any choice. Without the *Dauntless* we've got nothing. There's not enough trade comes through our neck of the woods for us to make a decent livin', not on the roads anyhow, and if'n we can't get to it in the skies it'll all go to the Riders, which we all know how much they like to share. If we don't have a ship we got nothin', not a pot to piss in nor a window to chuck it out of. We may as well hang up our swords right now, for all the good that they'll do us.

"Now that's fine with me, I got the Edge to keep me going, but what about the rest of you? How're you gonna make ends meet? Day jobs? You gonna find work down the slate mines, bending your backs from dawn 'til dusk for a handful of coin and a kick in the arse seven days a week? I don't think so." A couple of the men scowled at the very idea, that's when Fenris knew he had them. "I mean, maybe one of you could come work here for me, I needs me a new chamber maid to change the sheets and scrub out the chamber pots and that, but what about the rest of you? What are you gonna do to put food on the table and a smile of your wife's face, eh?"

The four men had a brief, silent discussion, communicating their concerns with tight lips, harsh looks, and a distinct desire to smash something in frustration. Fenris glanced up at his son who stood nearby, and tossed him a cheeky wink. He was clearly confident in the outcome, even if Toby wasn't.

Finally, somehow, by silent assent, Lazy Larry was chosen to speak for the group. "What did you have in mind?"

Chapter 7

When Bad Things Happen

John Sinister felt a hand on his shoulder. "Huh. Wassup? Woz-goin'on?"

"Time to go," whispered Billy.

John rolled out of bed reluctantly, dragging on his clothes with his eyes shut. There was no point in opening them, it was pitch black in the crew's quarters. And even if it wasn't, there was nothing interesting to look at anyway (although a little light would have made finding his boots a lot easier).

He found Billy in the galley, making a sandwich by candlelight. "It's gonna be a long day. You better make something for the road."

John contemplated the loaf of bread with little enthusiasm. "What time is it?"

"About five, five-thirty."

"Hell's teeth! That's the middle of the night."

"I told you, it's gonna be a long day. The sooner we get there the sooner we can get back. And you never know, there might be complications. We want to give ourselves as much leeway as we can."

"Complications? What sort of complications?"

Billy shrugged. "No idea. But when you're dealing with the reivers anything could happen. It's best to be prepared." He wrapped his sandwich in some parchment paper and stuffed it into his backpack, along with an apple, a pear, and a couple of samosas he'd found hiding under a cloth. "I'll see you up top," he said, heading for the door. "Don't forget that sandwich. You'll need it before the day is out."

Cursing under his breath, John hacked at the loaf with all the skill and petulance of a small child trying to sculpt a marble block with a feather duster.

John emerged onto the deck of the *Dragonfly* with a wedge of bread and jam stuffed in his pocket and a number of cuts on his hand, none of which were very deep but all of which he could have done without. The sun was just beginning to peek over the mountains, tinging the clear skies a deep smouldering red, and the still morning air was crisp and clean, both refreshing and annoyingly cold all at the same time. "Looks like a nice day for it," he said. "I thought it'd still be raining after last night."

"Nah. That's one good thing about the Lake District, if you don't like the weather just give it a minute, it'll change soon enough." Billy pointed towards a hill to the north. "That's where we're headed. The Western Riders are holed up in Rydal Caves. It's fairly flat most of the way, with a little uphill at the end. Are those new boots?"

"Newish. Why?"

"Are they worn in?"

"I'd say so, yeah."

"Coz it's a long way. If they're not worn in you'll get blisters."

"They're worn in."

"That's what all you city boys say, then it's all 'Ooh! Aah! Can we stop for a little while, my plates are barking.'"

John pursed his lips. "Look, don't you worry about me, mate, alright? I wasn't born with a silver spoon in my mouth. I know what's what."

"Great," said Billy, heading down the gangplank. "Then come, my friend, let us see what dwells amongst the untrodden ways."

"Yeah, right," said John, following on after him. "Whatever you say."

In the Western Riders' cave, the smell of porridge filled the air, as it did every morning (much to the annoyance of Magnus Sigurdsson).

"Porridge again? Can we not have some eggs or something?"

"Have you got any eggs?" said Molly, stirring the pot.

"No."

"Then shut up."

Magnus sipped at his tea noisily. Molly ignored him, even though every slurp went right through her.

Over on the *Molly's Kiss*, the lads were beginning to show a leg. They'd spent the night because retribution was coming, and they needed to be ready when it did, but how long could they keep that up? These men had families and homes of their own to protect. They couldn't stay up at the caves forever.

Molly passed her brother a bowl of porridge which he jabbed at sullenly. "What are we gonna do, Moll?"

"I don't know."

"We need a plan."

"I know."

"So what are we gonna do?"

"I don't know."

John's feet were killing him. Their civilised walk through town had been replaced by a long, uneven walk along the shore of the lake that, but for want of a steam roller and a couple of inches of tarmacadam, was actually quite lovely. The daffodils were out along the shoreline, the sun bounced lightly off the lapping waves, and the views you got of the surrounding hills and mountains filled your soul in a way you didn't get in your local park or recreation ground. If only the walk had been a bit easier.

There was actually a perfectly serviceable road a few hundred metres to their right, but Billy seemed to prefer the sand beneath his feet and the wind upon his face, so along the water's edge they went.

"How's it going back there?"

"Fine," said John.

"Once we reach the top of the lake we're almost there. We can have a break then. Unless you fancy a break before, that is? How're your feet holding up?"

John stumbled over a small rock. "Don't you worry about me, mate. I'm alright."

"Excellent," said Billy cheerily, without looking back. "At this pace we should be there in no time!"

Dexter followed Sue out of the cave, glad to get a little fresh air finally. He didn't know if she understood what was going on with the pirates (he could hear what they were saying, and even he was having trouble figuring it out), but he could tell she didn't like the funny mood everyone seemed to be in. He didn't blame her for wanting to be elsewhere.

Sue had a wooden ball with her, a poor man's cricket ball that was more splinter than paint these days, and a book about mushrooms and fungus that was on the verge of falling apart. Dexter figured she'd read that guy's lips or something, and was on her way to find something more interesting to cook for breakfast.

They left the cave via a series of stepping stones along the water's edge, emerging out onto a rocky plateau. Sue led Dexter down the hill a little to where a small wood began. Opening her book, she turned to a page full of illustrations and held it up for him to see. Tapping on two of the pictures – one that looked like an orange dinner plate and another that looked like an inside out yellow umbrella – she pointed at her eyes, then out at the woods. Dexter almost said 'Got it,' until he remembered he couldn't speak. Following Sue into the woods, he kept his eye out for any flashes of yellow or orange.

"How much farther?" said John.

"Not far now," said Billy.

"It was 'not far now' two 'not fars' ago," John grumbled .

Billy laughed. "Seriously, it's not too far now."

John and Billy were on a wide path heading uphill through some woodland. There was birdsong on the air, the faint sound of running water somewhere amongst the trees, and every now and then something small would shoot off into the undergrowth, too quick to see but clearly in a hurry to get somewhere less peopled as fast as non-humanly possible.

Scrambling up a section of path that looked suspiciously like a dried up river bed, they turned a corner and Billy stopped suddenly. Grabbing John he pushed him into the undergrowth, depositing him roughly in a shallow hole behind a large, scraggy gorse bush.

John, not being an idiot, didn't yell 'What the hell?!' or anything equally as asinine. Following Billy's worried gaze, he looked towards the top of the hill where the treeline ended and the path opened out onto a rocky hillside.

There were men in the woods, big men with swords and clubs and heaven knew what else. John spotted Michael from the Striding Edge amongst their number. The innkeeper had ditched his clean shirt and amiable demeanour in favour of a sheepskin waistcoat and the promise of extreme violence with a hint of death.

The men's attention was focussed on something beyond the brow of the hill, something which John assumed to be the Western Riders' hideout.

"It's the Wolves," whispered Billy. "Looks like they're gearing up for an attack."

"Then we need to get out of here, right?" said John. Billy said nothing. "Right?"

Billy pursed his lips.

"We need to warn the Riders."

"Oh no we do not," said John. "This is none of our business. Let 'em kill each other. What's it got to do with us?"

"It's *my* business," said Billy, looking for a way around the Northern Wolves. "Some of the Riders are... special to me."

"Special? Special how?"

"I'd rather not say," said Billy. *It's a girl,* thought John. *It's always about a girl.* "Look, you go back if you want to, but I'm going to warn the Riders that—" Billy's voiced choked off as a tiny figure stepped onto the path between them and the Northern Wolves. The bottom of her shirt pulled up so that she could cradle her bounty of mushrooms, Sue's attention was focussed solely on keeping her fungi in one place and not on anything else.

With careful and deliberate steps, she set off up the hill.

"This is bad," Billy whispered. "This is bad, this is bad, this is really, really bad."

A grey cat with a large mushroom in its mouth stepped onto the path behind Sue and followed her up the hill.

"You got that right," said John.

Toby squatted next to his father, wishing that he was anywhere else but there. He hadn't had much sleep. None of them had. The drinking had gone on until the wee hours, a deliberate ploy by his father to keep everybody in line, in place, and just the right amount of hung-over the next day to want to do violence to their fellow man. And it had worked too. Toby would have given anything to be home in bed right now, so much so he was tempted to stick his knife in his father's side, just to see what'd happen.

The plan, such as it was, was to nab one of the Western Riders when they came outside, preferably Molly Sigurdsson or her brother, Magnus, then exchange them for the *Molly's Kiss*, doing horrible things to their captive until the other Riders eventually complied. The idea of it turned Toby's stomach, but there was no point complaining. His father had been on the ragged edge since the *Dauntless* went down. He wouldn't recognise reason even if he could be made to see it.

Toby heard the footsteps at the same time as everyone else. He turned around and his heart sank. Beside him, his father chuckled.

"Well, well, well," said Fenris. "What do we have here?"

Billy could barely sit still. He wanted to rush out and grab Sue, but he thought that would only make a bad situation worse. "They wouldn't do anything to a little girl," he said, mostly to himself.

"The reivers aren't like that, not even the Wolves. It's all business with them, nothing personal. Right?"

John hesitated. "I'm sure you're right," he said. "Certainly seems that way anyhow." *And it better be,* he added mentally, *because God knows what Dexter'll do if they try anything.*

They watched Sue and Dexter pick their way up the rocky path, oblivious to the men in the woods around them. They passed the bulk of the group, none of the men doing anything to stop them, and were almost at the edge of the wood when Fenris Wolf stepped out in front of them and scooped up the little girl with one hand, sending her array of mushrooms tumbling to the ground.

"Oh Hell," whispered Billy, terror in his voice. "What'll we do? What'll we do? What'll we do?"

"I don't know," said John. "Just wait a moment."

John was watching Dexter, who in turn was watching the Northern Wolves. He looked ready to do something, although quite what was anyone's guess. But he was also smart enough not to escalate things if he didn't have to. They hadn't hurt the little girl, so as long as that remained the same he wouldn't do anything stupid to risk that happening. Probably.

Fenris Wolf passed Sue off to one of his men, issued some instructions, and the whole group set off back down the hill. Next to John, Billy started to panic.

"They're taking her! They're kidnapping Sue!"

John didn't hear him. His attention was on Dexter, who was following the Wolves down the hill, none of whom seemed to have noticed he was there.

"We can't let them take her! We can't. We can't let them do it!"

The group was coming closer to their hiding place. John figured he could grab Dexter as they passed by. If he was quick about it none of the Wolves would be any the wiser.

They came nearer. Sue squirmed as she tried to break free. She bit her captor on the hand and without thinking he clipped her on the side of the head hard enough for her to see stars. Screaming blue murder, Billy leapt from his hiding place, rushing the armed gang with nothing in his hands but hate and rage.

Launching himself at the man holding Sue, Billy punched him in the ear. The man yelled but didn't let go. Seizing the opportunity, Dexter leapt on the man's thigh and dug in all his claws, ripping at the man's leg like he was fluffing a pillow. The man squealed, pulling at Dexter with his free hand as he tried to fend Billy off with his free leg. "Th'hell?! Gerroffame ya– Hey! Giz a hand will ya!!" he yelled.

The rest of the Wolves moved in, one grabbing Billy whilst another tried to tackle the slashing ball of murder fur that was the enraged Dexter (of the two, he definitely drew the short straw).

A third man pulled a knife, pausing only long enough to decide who he was going to stick it in first.

"Bollocks," John moaned as he ran from cover. Grabbing a rock, he flung it at the knife-man. It bounced off the man's shoulder, drawing his attention but doing little else. Charging into the group, John started punching and kicking everything in sight. He knocked someone's knife to the ground. He picked it up. Something hit him in the head and he dropped the knife. Billy was on the floor being kicked. Dexter flew through the air. Someone shouted something psychotic (it may have been him). A man ran away with the little girl under his arm. John went after him. Someone grabbed the scruff of his neck. He fell back. There was a shadow, a fist, an explosion of light.

Then there was silence.

Dexter tumbled down the hillside, coming to a halt at the base of a tree. Stumbling to his feet, he looked around. There was the path, and there was Sinister lying face down on it, either dead or unconscious, it was hard to tell which. And there was Sue under the arm of some meat-head, being carried off to God knows where for God knows what reason.

He looked from one to the other, the dead man and the scared little girl, and made the only choice he could. Cutting through the trees, Dexter followed Sue and her captor down the wooded hillside.

As John slowly came round, a part of him began to wonder why his new choice of career required him to get knocked unconscious on such a regular basis.

"This one's waking up," said a faraway voice. John tried to focus on it but it wasn't easy. His brain was too busy trying to pass out for that to happen.

He felt a knife tip at his throat, right on the jugular. That focussed his attention right enough. "Where is she?"

"Who?" he managed, opening his eyes to a ring of cold, hard faces looming over him.

The knife tip pressed a little deeper. "The little girl. What have you done with her?"

The calmness with which the woman holding the knife spoke chilled John to the bone. He needed to choose his next words very carefully. Unfortunately, all he could think about was teeth and fur and sheep for some reason.

"Wolves," he managed. "She was taken by wolves."

The knife went from his throat. "Fenris. I knew it! I'll kill him. I'll kill the lot of 'em!!"

Whilst the woman – who bore a striking resemblance to the maid from the Striding Edge – explained in great detail what she was going to do the Northern Wolves, John took a look around his dank surroundings. He was in a cave, a surprisingly light and airy cave, most of which was taken up by the airship that had attacked the *Dragonfly*. His guide, Billy, lay next to him on the ground, beaten and bloody but still breathing thank the stars. He was being tended to by one of the pirates whilst the rest of them tried to restrain their leader from charging off on a murderous rampage. There were three of them and one of her, and still they were having a hard time of it.

John pushed himself up to sitting. "How's he doing?" he asked the little man tending to Billy.

"He'll live," the man said.

"Thank heaven for small mercies," said John, laying back down. His head was swimming.

"I guess," said the man, watching his mates trying to calm down the boss. John followed his gaze.

The pirate captain had a crossbow, a sword, a club and an axe, and she was trying to deposit them about her person so that she wouldn't have to leave any of them behind. One of the crew, a young guy about her own age, was talking to her but she didn't seem to be listening. Then he said something that caught her attention.

She looked over at John and his stomach tightened. There was a lot of rage behind those eyes, and it was all pointed in his direction. Putting down everything but the small hand axe, the woman came over to crouch next to John's head.

"You're going to tell me what happened, from who took the girl to what the hell you and Billy have to do with all this. And I swear to God, if I don't like any of your answers,"—she brandished the axe in front of John's face—"I'm gonna start chopping bits off of ya, d'ya understand?" John nodded dumbly. "Good. Now, tells us a story, and let's see how much of you is left by the time you finish."

Dexter had to run to keep up with the girl's kidnappers as they fled the scene of the crime. Tough though they obviously were, even they seemed to fear the wrath that would rain down on them once their nefarious deed was discovered. Only once they were down the hill, around the lake, through a wooded hillside and across a large, well-worn track, did they finally stop to get their breath back.

The man carrying Sue set her down next to a rock, whilst he went to get himself a drink of water. He didn't tell her to stay still. He didn't have to. The poor girl was too terrified to go anywhere.

Dexter snuck around behind the rock to where Sue sat with her knees drawn up to her chin, her arms wrapped tight around them. He nudged her thigh, just enough to get her to lift her head, and when she did the look in her eyes broke his heart. He'd never seen someone more afraid, or more certain that they were going to die. It made his blood boil. If he could have killed every one of those men there and then he would have, and he wouldn't have lost a moment's sleep over it either.

There was unease amongst the men. They exchanged unhappy looks, although none of them seemed willing to voice their concerns.

"What?" said the largest of the group, the one in the sheepskin vest. The other men avoided his gaze. "Come on, out with it. I can see you've got something to say."

"You never said nuthin' about kidnapping no kids, Fenris."

"I said we was gonna take hostages, din' I? What does it matter how old they are?"

"Because it's one thing takin' someone hostage, an' it's another when it's some wee bairn. It don't seem right somehow."

"Young, old, fat, thin. Whatever it takes to get us what we need I'm gonna do. You either get on board with that or you can sod off back to your brother's farm. I'm sure he's got a few tups you haven't put the wind up yet."

The man turned away, muttering, "T'ain't right, that's all I'm sayin'. T'ain't right at all."

The big guy, Fenris, turned to the youngest of the group. "Toby, you head back now and tell 'em we've got the girl and we're willing to swap her for the *Molly's Kiss*. Tell 'em we'll be up at the Striding Edge and to bring the ship up there soon as, like." He stepped closer to the boy and lowered his voice. Dexter had to strain to catch the next bit. "Tell them that if they don't bring the *Kiss* by sunset we'll kill the girl, got it? That she'll not be harmed before then, but once the sun goes down..."

The boy turned white as a sheet. His mouth moved up and down a few times. "But— But what about me, Dad? What'll they do to me when I tell 'em that?"

The big man smiled. "Don't you worry, son, you'll be fine. They wouldn't *dare* do anything to you. Not if they know what's good for them. Now off you go, there's a good lad. And don't forget, the Striding Edge before sunset, or else."

The young lad walked off, glancing back now and then only to get a reassuring wave from his giant of a father.

One of the other men sidled up to the big man. "They'll kill 'im, y'know, soon as look at him."

The big guy shrugged. "What happens happens. In the meantime, I've got a wee job for you."

Turning away in disgust, Dexter snuggled up next to Sue, climbing into her lap as much as he could with her knees drawn right up to her chin. He should have stayed out of sight, should have kept his head down, but he didn't care. He needed Sue to know she was not alone.

"You work for *who*?"

"The Venerable Society of Airships Owners, Sky Captains, and Itinerant Washerwomen. They hired me to find out why so much of their stuff was going missing."

"But we ain't been taking any more than normal," said the young man leaning against a nearby barrel. "Why should they start getting bothered now all of a sudden?"

"Because the Northern Wolves've been taking more'n their fair share, I reckon," said the woman sat within easy reach of John's throat. "Let me guess, this has all come about over the last six months or so?"

"Something like that, yeah," said John.

"See, Magnus, I *told* you the *Dauntless* was going out more than they was letting on. Fenris got greedy, and now we've got this numpty sniffing around. And he thinks he's the one should be in charge of everything, fer cryin' out loud."

The pirate captain stabbed her knife into the ground. John was so relieved she hadn't stuck it in him he decided not to take umbrage at being called a numpty.

Molly Sigurdsson pointed over at Billy, who lay unconscious still with a bloody rag tied to his head. "So that explains what you're doing here, but what about him? Why's he involved in all this?"

"I was hoping we could talk things through, maybe come to some sort of an arrangement. Billy there offered to show me where you lived."

"Did he now?" said Molly, looking unhappily in Billy's direction. She retrieved her knife from out of the ground. "That was stupid of him."

John had a horrible feeling in the pit of his stomach. "Yeah, well, he seems to make a habit of that. Like when he saw that little girl of yours in trouble. Ran straight in he did, to try and help her. Didn't think twice about it. Just charged in swinging and hoped for the best, poor bugger. He didn't stand a chance, but he did it anyway." John shrugged. "I guess he must think that wee girl of yours is pretty special or something."

The pirate captain considered Billy for an age. Wiping the dirt off her blade, she went to check on his wound, making sure the blanket they'd laid over him was tucked in nice and tight whilst she was there.

There was a commotion at the cave mouth. Raised voices and a scuffle. The two Jacks appeared, splashing through the water's edge, dragging an errant knave between them.

"Found this one sneaking around, boss," said one of the Jacks. They threw their captive at the captain's feet.

"I wasn't sneaking around," said Toby, rising to his knees. "I walked right up to your front door, plain as day."

Molly Sigurdsson grabbed Toby by the throat. "And why would you do something as stupid as that when you *know* you ain't walking out again?"

"Because I had to," gasped Toby. "I never got a choice."

Molly squeezed a little harder. Toby's face turned an unpleasant shade of purple.

"Perhaps we should hear him out," said Magnus. "He might have something important to say."

Molly Sigurdsson reluctantly let go of Toby's throat. "Go on then. What have you got to say for yourself?"

"Fenris has your little girl. He's willing to swap her for the *Molly's Kiss*. He wants you to bring the ship up to the Striding Edge before sundown or..."

"Or what?" Molly growled.

"Or you know what," said Toby, shaking his head. "My father is not a sane man, Moll, not anymore. Maybe he was once, but now... I dunno. There's no telling anymore. He might actually hurt that poor girl, if he thinks it'll get him what he wants."

Molly's knife was at Toby's throat quick as a flash. "If he does *anything* to our Sue I'll do the same to you, and that's a promise!"

Toby almost laughed. "You think that'll stop him? You think he cares what happens to me at all? You don't know what he's like. None of you do! The man's so full of cruelty and hate he wouldn't know happy if it came up and punched him in the face."

Molly saw tears in Toby's eyes. She stepped back and looked away, giving him the chance to wipe them away without the humiliation of having her see him do it. "You need to give him your ship, Molly. You need to give him your ship or he'll kill that little girl, sure as eggs is eggs." Toby sat back on his heels, his shoulders slumped. "I wish it weren't so but there it is. There's nothing else you can do."

Molly went quiet. She stared off into the distance. "What are you thinking?" asked Magnus.

"I'm thinking that even if we give Fenris the *Kiss* there's no way he's going to let us go. Whether it's today or tomorrow, he's going to have to deal with us eventually, so he'll do it today, because why wouldn't you."

"Yeah. That's the trouble with being a complete lunatic. You always have to go with the crazy option, no matter what. So what're we gonna do?"

"Fight, of course. Although God knows how. He'll see us coming a mile off up on that hill of his. And even if we could sneak up on him it'd be a bloodbath. We'd lose most of our lot, he'd lose most of his. And then there's Sue. I've no idea how we're going to get her out of there without her getting hurt somehow. The whole thing's a right mess."

"So let's give him the *Kiss* and hope for the best. If we can get out of there without a fight that may be the best we can hope for, for now. We can figure the rest out tomorrow."

"I don't want to give up the *Kiss*! Not to him."

"Neither do I. But we don't seem to have much choice in the matter, do we?"

John cleared his throat. "Actually," he said, his thoughts racing, "that's not entirely true." Everyone turned to look at John. "There is something you can do. Something that he's not gonna see coming, if you play your cards right."

"Go on," said Molly Sigurdsson. "I'm listening."

John swallowed loudly. "But before I tell you what it is, I have one condition."

Molly wagged her very pointy knife at John, "You're not really in a position to bargain, y'know."

John shrugged, conceding the point. "Nevertheless, if this works, you and I need to have a talk about you leaving the air couriers alone from now on. Deal?"

Molly grinned. "Mate, if you and I are both still alive when the sun goes down, we can have all the cosy fireside chats you like."

It took John just two minutes to outline his plan, but several hours for them to put it in motion. Men had to be sent to all corners of the Lake District to bring all the pieces together.

A message was sent to Shapside Stan to see if he could help, but it turned out Stan had problems of his own. He was in jail for trying to bribe a policeman who was either too honest for his own good or, more likely, thought he was worth more than the measly sum Stan had offered him to look the other way. Whichever it was, Stan was off the board for the time being, as were his men, since they were too busy dismantling the local jail brick by brick to lend Molly and her crew a helping hand.

The sun had dropped low by the time everything had been put in place. All that could be done had been done, and although victory was far from assured, they at least had a bit of a fighting chance now.

"I hope this plan of yours works," said Molly Sigurdsson.

John thought 'plan' was probably too strong a word for it. He would have gone with 'notion', or 'concept', or 'lunatic idea born of desperation'. "So do I," he said.

Molly turned to her crew. Her gaze was met by a gang of determined faces and a lot of swords, clubs, and knives. She nodded approvingly. "Right then!" she said. "Let's get this show on the road."

Chapter 8

To Helvellyn And Back

The *Molly's Kiss* slipped her moorings and slid from her hiding place, dropping down the hillside to the lake before turning north towards Helvellyn and the Striding Edge. Following the same line taken by the *Dragonfly* a few days earlier, she skirted over some scrub land and along another lake before heading up the long inclined valley to where the *Dragonfly* had made her dramatic run up the mountain. The *Kiss's* crew kept her close to the ground, not out of fear, as had the *Dragonfly*, but to gain what advantage they could over Fenris and whatever trap he had lying in wait for them. They had nothing to fear from any predators they might meet along the way. They were the predators.

Molly Sigurdsson didn't take the *Kiss* all the way up the valley. Drifting off to the right, she cut in between the low hills, following a footpath that rose up to a place called Grizedale Tarn at the base of Helvellyn (John would later learn that a tarn, of which there were many in the Lake District, was simply a small lake you found half way up a hill or mountain – although quite why such a thing needed its own name would remain a mystery to him). There they dropped their cargo before heading back west to the valley, so they could come at the inn from the expected direction and with the sun behind them. It also gave everybody time to get in place. Timing would be everything.

Carrying on up the valley, they reached its peak. Turning to face the mountain, Molly considered the way ahead before addressing the crew. "We'll be coming in high. There's no need for sneaking, they know we're coming. I'm not expecting any trouble from the skies but keep an eye out. Anyone spots anything they don't like give a yell. There's no prizes for keeping your mouth shut at a time like this." Giving the signal to toss some ballast over the side, Molly Sigurdsson set the *Kiss* soaring straight up into the air.

As they pulled level with the top of Helvellyn, the wind caught them, pushing them off course, but it was nothing the engine couldn't handle. Turning into the wind, Molly brought her ship in towards the inn. The sun was low on the horizon, giving the skies a rich orange glow that would have warmed your heart on any other night. Stood beside Molly at the wheel, John Sinister suddenly wondered how the hell he'd gotten himself in the middle of all this mess.

They came closer to the inn. "Looks deserted," said John.

Molly said nothing. She took the ship on a long wide sweep around the lone building. The inn's braziers stood cold and dark, its curtains drawn and its doors firmly shut. No ships stood at anchor, nor could they have with all the donkeys wandering about. Swinging round the back of the inn, they found the donkey pen dismantled, its long poles stacked up against the side of the building, its bales of hay heaped in one massive pile out in the open, next to a large rock.

John hadn't noticed before but the back of the inn was only fifty feet from a surprisingly perilous drop-off that fell away at a sharp angle to a large, deep, uninviting tarn far below. He hadn't noticed because it looked like your average grassy hillside from up top, but as Molly Sigurdsson positioned her ship close to the almost-a-cliff-but-not-quite's edge, and he got that tingling sensation in his nether regions, he could tell that like a lot of things around here it was a damn sight more treacherous that it at first appeared to be.

Molly turned to John. "You better get yourself ready." She went to the side of the ship. "Fenris! Get out here, NOW!" she roared. Nothing moved save for the nearest donkeys, who looked up lazily from their grazing to see what all the fuss was about. "I'm not playing, Fenris. Get out here or you're gonna regret it." Molly gestured for some of her crew to come forward. They dragged a broken figure between them, his head and shoulders covered in a hessian sack. "We've got your boy, Toby. If you don't come out right now,"—Molly nodded to the man at the wheel and the *Kiss* drifted away from the inn so that its entire body hung over the precipitous drop—"over the side he goes!" Throwing him against the ship's rail, the two men grabbed a leg each. Toby whimpered as his feet left the deck and all he could feel either end of him was cold fresh air and impending doom.

For the longest time, it looked like Fenris was going to let them kill his boy. John wondered what a fall like that would be like. If you would scream all the way down, or give in to the inevitability halfway through.

Eventually, the back door of the inn swung open and Fenris emerged, followed by three of his men. In amongst them came Sue, tiny by their side. She was blindfolded, her hands tied, her face streaked with tears.

No one saw the cat slip from the inn behind them.

"DAMN YOU, FENRIS!! You take that blindfold off her, NOW!!" Fenris sighed, but did as he was told. Molly waved to get Sue's attention. She placed both hands flat against her chest and then pulled them away into a thumbs up gesture. Sue nodded. Molly placed her hand by her ear like she was listening for something, twisting it forward in a kind of lazy salute. She made a pyramid with both her hands, followed by a fist that she turned into a half-complete thumbs up. Sue nodded again, but she didn't seem convinced. Molly turned her attention back to Fenris. The look on his face made her blood boil. It was a good job they were hanging over top of a very big drop. If she could have gone over the side and landed with her hands on Fenris's throat she would have.

"I'm glad you saw sense, Molly. I'd have hated to think that—"

"Shut up, Fenris! No one cares what you think. Kidnapping a child. I can't believe it. And *you*, Larry Latimer." Molly pointed at the man behind Sue, the one with his hand on her shoulder. "I never thought you'd be a part of this. You went to school with Sue's dad, fer crying out loud." Lazy Larry's chin dropped as he looked away. "You should be ashamed of yourselves. The whole lot of ya. Bloody ashamed!"

"Enough!" barked Fenris. He grabbed Sue and pulled her forward. "You didn't come here to watch your little girl die, so just land that thing and let's get this over with."

Molly glanced past Fenris to the path up from Grizedale Tarn. "How do I know I can trust you? How do I know you won't kill us soon as we land?"

Fenris laughed. "You don't. But I can promise you this,"—one of Fenris's men came round the side of the inn carrying a longbow, a flaming arrow nocked and ready to shoot—"if you *don't* come down here, right now, Sykes'll blow the lot've you to kingdom come. So what's it gonna be, Moll? You gonna set down, or are you gonna leave young Sue here all alone in the world?"

Molly gripped the ship's rail, twisting it like she was trying to break it in half. She pointed to a patch of grass next to where Fenris was standing and gestured angrily at the helmsman, the Northern Wolves making space as the *Kiss* manoeuvred into position. The ship dropped low enough to run out a gangplank and three figures descended – Molly Sigurdsson, her bother Magnus, and the man with the sack on his head. "We exchange hostages first," said Molly. "Once I have Sue the rest'll come down, not before."

Fenris nodded. "That's fair, I suppose." He pushed Sue towards Molly, the girl walking hesitantly forward. Molly kicked Toby in the backside and he stumbled forward too, tripping over the rocky ground like a drunken baby antelope.

The second she was within reach, Molly swept Sue up in her arms, the little girl burying her face into the crook of Molly's neck as hard as she possibly could. Her bound hands clung to Molly's arm, pulling herself closer as Molly squeezed and squeezed, using all her might to squeeze away the fear as best she could.

Toby reached his father only to be pushed roughly behind him, into the arms of Lazy Larry Latimer. Lazy Larry pulled the sack off Toby's head and made a confused sound. "Surprise!" exclaimed John, headbutting Lazy Larry square on the nose. Lazy Larry stumbled over backwards blood spurting through his filthy fingers as John, struggling to separate his bound hands, bolted for the nearest gap he could find.

"What the—"

"Now!" yelled Molly, running for cover with Sue in her arms as a great roar went up along the Grizedale Tarn trail.

Fenris and the Wolves spun round to see the crew of the *Molly's Kiss* charge onto the mountain, flanked either side by Billy and an out-of-uniform Constable Kent. They all had knives and clubs, and enough rage to last a lifetime, and they sprinted towards the Northern Wolves as if they'd just had to hike up a mountain in double time and they needed someone to take it out on.

On the *Molly's Kiss,* the crew of the *Dragonfly* threw off their disguises and readied for battle, Captain Tonbo staying at the wheel whilst the rest of them prepared to charge down the gangplank.

"Now!" yelled Fenris at the big pile of hay.

The haybale twisted round, clunked loudly, and a massive iron bolt shot from its side, a thick line of rope trailing through the air behind it. It punched a hole in the hull of the *Kiss*. Captain Tonbo instinctively tried to fly away, lunging for the open skies, but it was no use. The iron teeth of the harpoon dug into the ship's wood, its rope drew tight, and with a series of inexorable clicks, the Long South's harpoon began drawing the *Molly's Kiss* in towards the cold, hard earth.

Little Neck of Ecclefechan stuck his head out of the pile of hay. "Gotcha, ya bastard!" he crowed. "Right lads! Have at 'em. You know what to do!"

Four figures with crossbows appeared on the roof of the Striding Edge. Bracing themselves against the slippery straw as best they could, they opened fire on the *Kiss*, sending the crew of the *Dragonfly* diving for cover as they rained a hail of crossbow bolts down upon them.

The Northern Wolves charged to meet their attackers head on. Their assailants were tired, and for the most part smaller than them, but what they lacked in height they made up for in enthusiasm. Billy nearly blinded one man, swinging his walking stick around his head, whilst Snick the Thief did some serious damage to the Tup Worrier, a man twice his size, by running up his body and pounding on his face with a rock he'd picked up along the way. It took both of the Jacks to keep Fenris busy, leaving Lazy Larry to find out what the business end of a police constable's cane felt like.

Dexter found John Sinister on his knees by a not very sharp rock trying to cut the ropes around his hands. "Alright, Meat, need a hand?"

"I told Magnus not to tie them too tight," said John, holding out his hands. "Either he's better at knots than he thinks he is, or he's much, much worse."

Dexter cut through the ropes with one of his steel claws.

"Where's the girl?"

John pointed over to where the airships would normally land. "She's safe. Her mum's getting her out of the way."

"Good. So now what?"

John scoured the battlefield. He pointed at the man by the side of the inn, who was looking for something unpleasant to do with his flaming arrow. "Can you take care of that whilst I take care of the harpoon?"

"Done and done," said Dexter, charging off at full pelt.

Aboard the *Kiss*, Captain Tonbo gunned the engines, trying to break free from the harpoon. It was no use. Click by inevitable click the harpoon's winch pulled the airship closer to the ground.

They were still too high for anyone to jump down and join the fight though, a fact which enraged an already thoroughly enraged Mento Jones. "I can make it," he growled.

"No you can't," said Agnes. "You'll break your leg."

"I can make it! I've done it before."

"No you haven't."

"He has actually," interjected Jacko. "It wasn't pretty."

"I'm telling you, I can—" Jones caught sight of something that made his blood run cold.

Mrs Mulligan appeared at the back door of the inn, ladle in hand, ready to give some noisy bugger a right good telling off. Taking one look at the bloody chaos she quickly retreated back inside, bolting the door behind her as if that would do any good.

"No," Jones snarled angrily. "Not on my watch."

"Eh?" said Agnes. "What do you– No, wait!"

Breaking cover, Mento Jones rushed the length of the ship, crossbow bolts dogging his every step. He launched himself off the back of the boat screaming, his father's leather apron (along with a few other things his father had given him) flapping in the wind. There was nothing between him and the ground but gravity; gravity, and the rope leading up from the harpoon to the hull of the *Molly's Kiss*. Jones landed on the thick rope, the bottom of his leather apron somehow getting in between it and his hands, and with a yell of triumph he slid all the way down the rope to good old terra firma.

Jones couldn't see anything with his father's apron up around his head, but down by the harpoon, Little Neck of Ecclefechan saw it all, mostly because what he saw was hurtling towards him at a very high rate of knots. "Boggin' bawbags!" he exclaimed as the sweaty bottom half of Mento Jones slammed him in the face, knocking him into merciful unconsciousness. Scrambling to his feet, Mr Jones adjusted his apron, found his meat tenderiser, and with a roar of triumph started bashing his way through the crowd towards the back door of the Striding Edge.

Well that solves that problem, thought John, regarding the mangled pile of Border Reiver. *Now, what to do about this rope?*

By the side of the inn, Dexter launched himself at the man with the flaming arrow. Running up his leg, he sank his steel claws deep into what was fast becoming his favourite place to grab people. The man, Sykes, screamed and arched backwards, loosing the flaming arrow high into the air. Dexter ripped his paw away, holding tight to everything the man held dear, and Sykes crumpled to the ground, whimpering.

The Long Souths on the roof of the inn were having the time of their lives. They hadn't been involved in a fight like this, a full-on scrap that they could really sink their teeth into, in what felt like forever.

As a rule, people avoided the Long Souths if at all possible. The Souths liked to think it was because they were such fierce fighters that all the other clans were afraid of them, but that was not the case. To a man (or woman, the Long Souths being far more concerned about how someone handled themselves in a fight than with what went on between their legs) the Souths had such a love of strong garlic, boiled cabbage, and cheap gin – and such an aversion to soap and water – that being in the same room as them was enough to make your eyes water. They could clear a pub in a matter of seconds – even one full of tanners, knackers, sheep farmers, and soil men – and if you were unfortunate enough to have to entertain one of their number in your enclosed carriage you'd be airing that thing out for a month.

The only good thing about the Long Souths was that it was very hard for them to sneak up on you in the dark, which was why they were making the most of the opportunity to hurt people while they could. The Souths liked hurting people, and if they could hurt people without getting hurt themselves, even better.

So intent were they on making sure their crossbow bolts found their targets, they failed to notice the flaming arrow that fell from the sky, lodging itself deep into the thatched roof behind them.

Molly sat Sue down next to one of the iron hoops where the airships normally came in to land. Going down on one knee, she kissed the little girl on the forehead and signed, *Stay here. I'll be back.* Sue stared at her blankly. Molly looked over her shoulder to where the fighting raged. Things were getting messy. Her ship had been harpooned and her men were getting a bit of a pasting. She had to help them.

Molly ran towards the inn, but then stopped. She looked back at Sue, all alone on the muddy ground. She took a step towards her. Someone cried out. Molly turned back towards the fight. Then back to Sue. Then back towards the fight.

This was madness! What was she doing? It was Sue. This was all about Sue. She had to be kept safe.

Molly took a few steps towards Sue but then stopped, as all the donkeys that had been wandering about suddenly gathered around her. One of them snuffled Sue gently in the side of the head whilst another, the crotchety old mother donkey that never let anyone pet her, not even Sue, turned to Molly and abruptly tossed its head as if to say, 'Howay wid ya, lass. We got this.'

Molly blinked. She looked round the protective ring of donkeys. Was this real? Was this really happening? As if reading her mind, the mother donkey tossed its head again, stamping its foot to drive home the point.

This is crazy, thought Molly, drawing her sword. Nodding back at the mother donkey, she charged off into the fray.

John stared at the harpoon's winching mechanism, because if he stared at it long enough it was bound to make sense eventually, right? Where the hell was the brake? It had to be somewhere. He pulled in vain on a few of the levers but they wouldn't budge. The winch's wheel with its thick coil of rope wasn't going anywhere. John turned his attention to the rope itself. It was worn and weary, and weathered from use. He went for his knife only to find it gone. *Damn! Where the hell's that got to?* He made a futile search of the ground nearby, but all he found there was dust and dirt.

John glanced up to the roof of the inn, where a small fire was developing nicely. *Now* there's *an idea,* he thought.

Turning back to the machine, and the great handfuls of hay all around, John pulled a box of matches from his jacket pocket.

On the roof, the Long Souths were starting to notice how much warmer it had become. And lighter. And decidedly more smoky. They turned to discover the entire roof behind them solidly ablaze.

"Hell's teeth!" said one.

"God damn!" said another.

"Neuk dit! Ik ben weg hier," said a third with long blonde hair, throwing down his crossbow. His friends looked at one another.

"Did you know Charlie was Dutch?"

"Dutch? I didn't even know Charlie was a he."

They watched as Charlie ran down the inn roof. Grabbing onto one of the long poles leaning against the side of the building, he launched himself into the air, scrambling up the pole as it tilted forward towards the *Molly's Kiss*. He reached the top just as the pole hit the side of the ship, flinging him unceremoniously onto its deck. Pulling a knife, Charlie threw himself at the nearest man he could find.

Back on the roof, the remaining Long Souths were speechless.

"Did you know he could do that?"

"I didn't know *anyone* could do that."

"Could *you* do that?"

"I dunno," said the man, glancing at the flames behind them. "But I think we better find out."

Grabbing a pole each, the remaining Long Souths launched themselves off the roof of the inn.

On the deck of the *Molly's Kiss,* Agnes Goodenough peeked out from behind her bolt-riddled barrel to find that the fight was coming to her. "Finally," she said, stepping out into the open. "My turn."

The fight by the side of the inn had developed into a bit of a free-for-all. The fighters had gone from hitting one specific person to hitting whoever happened to be front of them, which meant that more than once someone they might have considered a friend caught an elbow to the face or a knee to the groin that they probably shouldn't have (The local clansmen had such a long history that they always had a reason to punch someone, even their nearest and dearest, but for now they were trying to stick to their respective sides for the most part).

Fenris Wolf picked up one of the two Jacks and flung him at the other one. He saw the roof of the inn on fire, Little Neck's harpoon on fire, and the Long Souths vault their way over to the *Kiss*. Determined to make sure it was the Northern Wolves and not the Long Souths who laid claim to the airship, he set off running.

Molly Sigurdsson reached the back of the inn just as Fenris Wolf came charging across her path. Flinging her sword at him to slow his run, she angled to intercept, grabbing on to Fenris as he grabbed on to the rope securing the *Kiss* to the flaming harpoon. Fenris tried to climb as Molly punched him in the back of the head, roaring in frustration as she lay into him. Wrapping his leg around the rope, he elbowed Molly in the face, catching her three hard blows before she lost her grip and fell to the ground.

Leaping to her feet, Molly ran for the harpoon, but as she grabbed for the rope it broke, its flaming end lifting swiftly yet inexorably beyond reach.

Molly screamed up at Fenris Wolf. "You're a dead man, Fenris. You hear me? DEAD!"

Halfway up the burning rope, Fenris stopped long enough to laugh triumphantly before casually making his way hand over hand to the deck of the *Molly's Kiss*.

At the helm, Captain Tonbo felt the ship break free. She also felt the dead weight dragging it over to one side. Swinging the ship around to keep it close to the ground, she risked glancing over the side to see what it was that was weighing them down.

On deck, Agnes was just getting into the swing of things (literally swinging one of the Long Souths around by their legs) when she heard the captain cry out, "Agnes!" She turned to see Fenris Wolf climbing over the side of the airship. Running round to the foot of the quarterdeck, Agnes got herself in between Fenris and the captain just as his size thirteens hit the woodwork.

There's a phrase, toeing the line, which people think comes from boxing, but it doesn't. The phrase used in boxing, according to the London Prize Ring Rules, is toeing the scratch. Fighters would stand at a line scratched into the ground, beating the hell out of each other until one of them went down, gave up, or they all got arrested by the police. It was a nasty, bloody way to run a legitimate fight, but until someone came up with something better (there were rumours a Welshman by the name of Chambers was working on something) they were the only rules they had.

Agnes was aware of the shortcomings of the London Rules. She had been forced to toe the scratch more than once in her life before now. But she was also aware that if you knew what you were doing there were certain advantages to be had too; especially if the moron you were facing off against thought you were about to fight fair.

Stretching out her foot, Agnes drew an imaginary line on the deck. Adopting the traditional fighting stance, she cocked her head to one side. It took Fenris a moment to twig what was going on.

Raising his fists, Fenris stepped up to the scratch, grinning. "I'm gonna beat you like a red-headed step-child," he growled.

Agnes chuckled. "Mate, you couldn't beat a rotten egg."

Agnes jabbed twice with her left, then threw a wild haymaker any pugilist worth their salt would see coming a mile off. Fenris duly ducked. Agnes stomped on his foot, kicked his knee sideways, and threw herself on top of him as he fell to the ground, getting in as many elbows as she could before he knew what hit him.

Captain Tonbo watched as Fenris caught Agnes a rattling blow, knocking her to one side. She saw her husband and Jacko cornered by the Long Souths, holding their own but not for long. The outcome was inevitable. They needed more help or they were going to lose the ship. Angling her nose down, Captain Tonbo sent the *Kiss* plunging towards the ground.

By the side of the inn, the fight had reached its natural resting point. It was still ongoing, no one had given up, but a lot of people were standing with their hands on their knees, panting.

"I'm surprised at you, Larry," gasped Constable Kent. "I never thought you'd be involved in owt like this."

Lazy Larry shook his head. "I know, I know. I don't like it any-mor'n you. But he's the guvnor, inne. I got no choice."

"There's always a choice, you know that."

"Easy for you to say, you don't—" A dark shadow fell across the two men. They dove to the side as the prow of the *Kiss* dug a deep groove in the earth right where they'd been standing.

On the deck of the ship, everyone who didn't have their sea legs was thrown to the ground. Captain Tonbo waved to Mick and Jacko. "Lines over the side! Get the crew on board!"

Running the length of the ship, Mick and Jacko tossed what ropes they could over the rail, managing a couple either side before the Long Souths laid into them again.

On the ground, the Northern Wolves and the Western Riders fought for the trailing lines, chasing after the ship as it scraped along the mountain top. They punched and kicked as they climbed the lines, men falling by the wayside until just two of them had managed to climb on board. Captain Tonbo steered the ship up into the air and found to her dismay that the two men who had made it were both faces she did not recognise.

Throwing Agnes into the arms of his men, Fenris turned his attention to Captain Tonbo. "It's over, Captain. The ship is ours. Put her down and you and your men can go free. Don't,"—Fenris looked to where the Long Souths had Mick and Jacko at knife point—"and I guarantee you won't like what happens next."

Captain Tonbo's eyes swept the deck. She gave a short, sharp nod. Turning the ship back round towards the inn, she brought it in gracefully over the flat space behind the inn's back door.

The Long Souths lined up at the ship's rail, crossbows in hand, keeping those on the ground at bay whilst Mick, Jacko, and Agnes jumped to safety. There was no one left to climb on board. Lazy Larry had decided he'd had enough for one night, Sykes it seemed had done a runner, and no one was interested in lifting an unconscious Little Neck to safety. Only when all her crew had safely disembarked did Captain Tonbo leave the ship, leaping one-handed over the railing to land with an impressive roll to standing when she hit the ground.

Fenris swung the ship around, bringing it to rest safely out of reach just beyond the cliff edge. He took in his vanquished foes, framed by the light of the Striding Edge. The inn was comfortably ablaze, and well on its way to becoming a burnt-out shell. "Don't feel bad, Molly," he yelled. "You tried your best. You and yours fought hard, but in the end you were no match for the Northern Wolves."

"En het Lange Zuiden," someone added in a Dutch accent.

"Indeed," said Fenris, frowning. "Anyway, to show there's no hard feelings why don't you take the Striding Edge as compensation. It's a fair swap, my inn for your ship. What do you say, Molly? Does that sound fair to you? Molly? Where are you, damn it?"

Molly Sigurdsson climbed atop a large rock. She held Sykes's bow in her hand, a flaming arrow nocked and ready to shoot.

"Sounds fair to me," said Molly. "Now how's about a little going away present, to show there's no hard feelings?" Molly drew her bow and pointed it at the ship's enormous balloon.

"No! Don't you dare!" screamed Fenris, yanking at the ship's controls. Molly smiled up at him. She loosed her arrow with a melodic twang and the flaming bolt sailed through the air, a shooting star of death and destruction. It punched a hole in the side of the balloon, disappearing from view like a match dropped in the ocean.

From deep within there came a faint *whumf*, far away and ominous.

Flames shot out of the small hole, ripping swiftly outwards to engulf the entire balloon. Men screamed as the *Molly's Kiss* fell from the sky, a boat with no ocean dragging a flaming ball of death in its wake.

The ship slammed into the grassy mountainside. Turning to slide down the near vertical cliff, she smashed into rocks and ridges as she hurtled to her doom. Her balloon collapsed down on top of her, men screaming in agony as the flaming canvas wrapped itself around them. Bouncing down the mountainside, the ship did her best to come apart as she hurtled towards the small lake far below.

There was no hope in the lake, with its promise to quench the flame, and no hope for Fenris and his men. The *Molly's Kiss* slammed into its unforgiving waters, smashing into a thousand pieces. The bits that didn't sink set on fire, and as the screams of the men were replaced by the pop and whine of old tar giving itself up to the inevitable, a funeral pyre of wood and canvas settled near the water's edge.

On top of the mountain, with the Striding Edge burning behind them and the *Molly's Kiss* burning down below, the survivors of the battle looked on in silence.

"Shouldn't someone say summink," said Lazy Larry. "Fer posterity, like."

Molly Sigurdsson spat over the side. "Good riddance to bad rubbish, that's what I say." Tossing her bow to the ground, she went looking for little Sue.

The rest of the group went off to lick their wounds, leaving just John and Larry to ponder over the flaming wreckage. Lazy Larry sighed. "Well, that's the end of the Northern Wolves, I reckon. I doubt young Toby will... Where is Toby anyhow?"

"He's back at the Riders' cave," said John. "He promised to cook everyone dinner if we didn't kill him."

"Aye, he always was more of a chef than a thief, that one."

"Wonder what he'll say when he finds out his dad is dead."

Something on the *Molly's Kiss* went bang, throwing a ball of flame high into the air.

"Not a lot, I reckon," said Larry. "They weren't exactly what you would call close."

Molly found Sue right where she'd left her, in amongst the donkeys. Sat next to her she also found an exhausted Billy, clinging on to both consciousness and Sue's hand with grim determination. The body of Sykes, the missing Wolf, lay nearby, beaten to death by someone who'd clearly fought for their life. Their life, or someone else's.

"What happened here?" said Molly.

Billy shrugged. "I saw Sykes go after Sue so I– I took care of it."

Molly knelt down in front of Sue. *Are you okay?* she signed. Sue signed back, pointing between Sykes and Billy. She made some strange gestures Billy didn't recognise – cupping her hand over a flat palm, pointing to herself, then placing both hands by the side of her mouth and pushing outwards, almost like she was shouting – ending by pulling herself closer to Billy's side. "What did she say?" he asked. Molly gave a half smile.

"What you said, more or less." Molly held out her hand. "Come on, Sue. Let's go home." Sue took her hand and the two of them stood, leaving Billy on his own in the mud and dirt.

Billy's head slumped as the exhaustion hit him. He was tempted to fall asleep right there, despite how filthy it was.

"You coming?" said Molly.

Billy looked up to find Molly holding out her other hand. Taking it, he pushed himself to his feet, fully expecting her to let go the second he was upright. But she didn't.

Hand in hand, watched approvingly by a phalanx of donkeys, the three of them walked off together across the muddy mountain-side.

CHAPTER 9

CHANGE IS GOOD...

Sat atop a bundle of freshly-cut thatch, John and Dexter watched with great amusement as a group of local lads struggled to manoeuvre the last of the hydrogen carts along the waterfront to the awaiting *Dragonfly*. Every time it hit a rut or pebble it tried to fly away, the lads leaping into action to drag it back down to earth whilst the donkeys tried to figure out why their back legs were suddenly flailing about in mid-air.

"So it turns out that tying a large balloon of floating gas to a small wooden cart pulled by a couple of moody donkeys makes it difficult to handle," said Dexter. "Well who knew!"

"What gets me is how the hell did they get it down the mountain?" John replied. "Did they fly it down or what?"

"Your guess is as good as mine, Meat. Maybe ask Billy later. I'm sure he'd be happy to fill you in." Billy had been put in charge of refilling the *Dragonfly's* new gleaming white canvas balloon. He hadn't wanted to do it of course, he wasn't an idiot, but if it meant the airship would be able to fly the thatch they needed to rebuild the Striding Edge up the mountain then he was willing to give it a try. After all, getting hydrogen down the mountain was a damn site easier than getting thatch up it (just about).

"I'm surprised they managed to get the repairs done so quickly," said John. "Two days and there she is, all fixed up and raring to go."

"Yeah, you meat-sacks really know how to get on with things when you put your mind to it," said Dexter.

Securing the cart to the dockside, Billy and his men set about filling the already almost full balloon with the last load of hydrogen gas.

Captain Tonbo came down the gangplank to keep an eye on things. She spotted John sitting on the pile of hay. "Ah, Mr Sinister. You are finished with the local constabulary, I see. Will you be joining us on our maiden voyage up to the Striding Edge?"

"I will, Captain, yes. And Constable Kent would like to come along too, if that's alright? He has a few things to clear up before he submits his final report."

"So long as he is here when we leave he is most welcome. I have no intention on waiting on any passengers. We have wasted enough time as it is. We need to head south and start earning money. There are bills to pay, you know."

Constable Kent arrived as they were cramming the last of the Striding Edge's wood and thatch into the *Dragonfly's* hold.

"Just in time, Constable. We were about to leave without you."

"Thank you for the ride, Captain. It's much appreciated. The Lake District may be a beautiful place to live, but you do get sick of going up and down these damn hills all the time."

The constable joined Captain Tonbo on the quarterdeck, so they could clear up a few details about recent events along the way, whilst John found Billy on the forecastle, eagerly anticipating the coming journey.

"This is my first time on an airship, you know," said Billy. "I'm rather looking forward to it."

"Well let's hope the captain can get her in the air then," said John. "That's a lot of weight we took on board."

Casting off from the dock, Captain Tonbo steered the *Dragonfly* away from shore. All the ballast they'd taken on during the rebuild had been dumped, but even so the captain had to steer out to the centre of the lake, where there was a decent headwind, before she was able to take to the skies once more.

A sudden gust and the *Dragonfly* rose into the air, turning to follow the shoreline north as she made for the Striding Edge. Hundreds of daffodils lined the lake's edge, a shimmering streak of gold and yellow dancing lightly in the waves of wind. Billy leant over the side of the ship, his eyes wide. "Gosh, look at them all. I've never seen so many! How majestic they look, tossing their heads in sprightly dance. How magnificent. Truly a more blissful sight ne'er there was."

"Whatever floats your boat, mate," said John, who wasn't really listening.

"How like a single host they look. And how like a cloud we must appear to them, floating high o'er hill and vale. Does it not fill your heart to be in such jocund company?"

"If you say so, pal," John replied, edging away from Billy before he burst into song or something.

Leaving the lake and its daffodils far behind, the *Dragonfly* soon approached the top of Helvellyn, and what was left of the Striding Edge.

At first glance, other than the fact that it was missing its roof, the inn looked much as it always had. It was only when the airship flew over top that they saw what a shell of its former self it had become.

Everything wooden within its four walls, including the entire first floor, had been burnt to a crisp. Little remained save for some stairs leading up to nothing, the fireplace (ironically enough), and the cast iron range on which Mrs Mulligan had cooked her wonderful roast a few days earlier. Everything else now lay in a charred pile of wood and ash on the inn's front lawn, awaiting its removal down the mountain.

"Quite a mess," said Constable Kent, joining John at the ship's rail.

"You can say that again," John replied. "I'm surprised the place is still standing, to be honest."

"Aye well, Molly got lucky in that respect. The Striding Edge was built to last. It'll take more than a lick of flame to finish her off."

"I heard they're thinking about opening up to tourists, offering them donkey rides across the fells, that kind of thing."

"If they can get the donkeys to cooperate I think it's a great idea. Folks'll pay handsomely for an authentic bit of lakeland hospitality, I reckon, 'specially if someone else is doing all the walking on their behalf."

"So you're okay with the Western Riders taking over the running of the inn? The law, I mean, after everything that's happened?"

Constable Kent shrugged. "Why wouldn't I be? Fenris gave Molly the Striding Edge in exchange for her ship of his own free will. I was there when he did it. The fact that half that trade fell off a mountain in a ball of flame moments later is neither one way of the other. A trade was made, fair and square. As far as the law is concerned that's all there is to it, and anyone who says otherwise can take it up with the Riders themselves. Although, quite frankly, I wouldn't recommend it."

Scattering a smattering of grazing donkeys as she came in to land, the *Dragonfly* tied up next to the inn. They ran out the gangplank, to be greeted on the ground by Agnes Goodenough and Molly Sigurdsson.

Having nothing else to do whilst the *Dragonfly* was being made airworthy, Agnes had been helping out with the rebuild. With her sleeves rolled up and a shovel slung over one shoulder she looked at home amongst all the honest hard work that needed to be done. "Wotcha, Sinister. You finally come to give us a hand or what?"

"No chance," said John. "I'm just here to make sure you lot don't run out of things to hit with a hammer. Soon as this lot is unloaded I'm catching a ride back to civilisation where I belong. Speaking of which, you better get your stuff together if you're coming with us."

"Actually, I thought I'd stick around here for a bit longer, if that's alright with you, Moll? I'm rather enjoying all the fresh air and that."

"Of course, Agnes," said Molly. "You're welcome to stay as long as you want."

"You're sure?" said John. "Looks like a lot of hard work to me."

Agnes laughed. "Oh it is, no doubt about that. But it's fun nonetheless. And you can't fault the view, can you."

John took in all the lakes and mountains that surrounded them. In the bright morning sun, under the clear blue sky, it was a scene to gladden even the most cynical of hearts. "No you can't," he said.

Captain Tonbo came down the gangplank. "Miss Dexter, where is Mr Jones? We must see about removing his things from the ship as soon as possible, so that Mr Wolf can become acquainted with his new home."

"Oh, he's yon side of the inn cooking a farewell feast with the, um, future Mrs Jones," said Agnes, watching the captain's inscrutable face warily.

One of the unexpected consequences of what people had taken to calling The Battle of Striding Edge was the cementing of the romance between Mr Jones and the inn's cook Mrs Mulligan. Apparently he had rescued her from the burning building moments before the roof's inevitable collapse, an act for which she had been extremely grateful. In expressing her gratitude in food, praise, and a number of other ways, the two of them had become inseparable, culminating in Mr Jones popping the question unexpectedly (for him too) one intimate evening when the moon was as full and fulsome as his belly and when he found himself in the warm embrace of Mrs Mulligan's solid silver serving ladle. Mr Jones didn't know much, but he did know that when you find someone willing to let you be the little spoon you hang on to that woman with all your might.

Captain Tonbo wasn't happy with the turn of events but what could you do? Crew came and went. Such was the way of things. And she'd been able to replace Mr Jones almost immediately with young Toby Wolf, whose culinary skills, whilst still a little raw, were more than enough for their needs, so really she had nothing to complain about. Still, she would miss Mr Jones's vegetable samosas. And his Moroccan tagine. And his pies. And his puddings. And that thing he did with coconut and mint that used to melt in your mouth. But apart from all that, she wouldn't miss him one bit.

"'Yon side of the inn'?" said John, smiling. "Have you gone native on us or what?"

Agnes punched John in the arm playfully, nearly knocking him to the ground.

Down the gangplank came Billy carrying two large boxes of nails. He walked over to Molly Sigurdsson, who looked both pleased and embarrassed to see him. "We managed to get everything we need on board," he said. "I'll go get the lads and we can start unloading."

"Thank you, Billy," said Molly, squeezing his arm tenderly. "It's, um, nice to have you back."

Billy blushed. He seemed uncertain whether to stay or go, lunging in to kiss Molly on the cheek then scurrying away with his boxes of nails before anyone could comment.

John's eyebrows shot up. It seemed Mr Jones' and Mrs Mulligan's wasn't the only blossoming romance on the top of Helvellyn that day. Molly shot John a look, daring him to say something funny, but he very quickly found something else to stare at instead.

Sue came over and stood next to Molly. Seeing her, Dexter came down off the ship to say hello. "So, this is the illustrious Dexter," said Molly Sigurdsson. "He must be very special for you to have risked your life to get him back."

"I wouldn't say that," said John, catching a scathing look from Dexter. "But he has his moments."

Sue tugged on Molly's sleeve, miming something that looked like cat's whiskers followed by a repeated two-fingered pinching gesture by the side of her mouth. Molly gave her a questioning look, chopping her hand into a flat palm. Sue nodded back emphatically. "What's going on?" said John.

"Sue says your cat can talk," said Molly, locking eyes with Dexter.

John started to splutter. "Talk! Him? Good Lord, no. Where'd she get an idea like that?"

Molly signed something to Sue, and Sue signed something back. The longer the conversation went on the more John started to sweat. "She says you can see his lips move, that he only does it when he thinks no one is watching, and that he mostly makes sarcastic comments at other people's expense. That sound about right to you?"

John chuckled a fake laugh that was fooling nobody. "Oh come on now, whoever heard of such a thing. What an imagination she must have."

"Not really, no," said Molly.

"Oh come on, Sinister," said Agnes. "Of course he can talk. It's obvious. The two of you have been yacking away to each other ever since we set off. I'm surprised the whole world doesn't know by now. Seriously, if you two had wanted to keep it a secret you should have been a bit more discreet about it, don't you think?"

John looked down at Dexter, who seemed to shrug back in return.

"Well, I guess the cat's out of the bag," said Dexter.

"What the hell!" said Molly, taking a step back.

"Told you," said Agnes, smiling.

"To be honest with you, I'm glad," said Dexter. "Can you imagine what it's like only having this one to talk to all the time?" He nodded dismissively towards John. "It'll be nice to have someone new to talk to once in a while."

"So what now?" said John.

"Now? Now I'm going to freak a bunch of people out," said Dexter. He turned to Sue. "Want to come with me?" Sue nodded, and the two of them walked off towards the inn together.

Agnes and Molly went to help with unloading the cargo, leaving John to wonder what was going to happen next. If Dexter could talk freely in front of other people there'd be no shutting him up. No more being the silent partner, he'd expect to take an active part in every investigation from now on. Questioning witnesses, interrogating suspects, there'd be no stopping him. John shuddered as he realised just how difficult his already difficult life was about to become.

After carrying wood for a few minutes because he felt guilty watching everyone else hard at work, John found himself a nice out of the way spot behind some bundles of thatch to wait until the food was ready. He was just getting comfortable when Mick the Spanner appeared looking furtive.

Mick froze when he saw John. "Sorry. I was looking for, um…"

John tapped the side of his nose. "I ain't seen you if you ain't seen me. Deal?"

"Deal," said Mick, squatting down out of sight beside John. "I love my wife more than anything but she's got a real bee in her bonnet about losing Mr Jones. If I have to listen to her list any more foods she's going to miss I'll go spare."

"Aye, it'll be a loss to the ship and no mistake, but I'm sure Toby'll do fine. That meal he made us the day of the fight was top notch."

"I'm sure too, but it doesn't stop the captain complaining about it any less."

The two men sat in silence, watching far away clouds drift across the horizon.

"So," Mick began, "that cat of yours can talk."

"I'm afraid so."

"Amazing. Truly amazing. I mean, it was just a matter of time before they made automatons that were more, er, autonomous, but still…"

John sighed. "Yup. It's a modern miracle and no mistake."

"What's he like to work for?"

"Excuse me?"

"He's been going round telling everyone you work for him."

"I don't work for him, no."

"But he's the legal owner of Chard Mechanical, right? That's what he's been saying."

"He is, but I don't work for Chard Mechanical either. I'm my own man, and Dexter, Dexter's my temporary associate. And he's getting more temporary by the second."

"Oh. I see."

John sat back and closed his eyes, as the two men lapsed into silence once more. Mick cast John a sideways glance. "So I guess your work is done now, now that all the pirate ships have been destroyed?"

"Looks like it."

"Did you, er, did you ever figure out what was going on with the pirates? How they were getting their information, I mean."

"Oh yes," said John. "Yes, indeed I did."

"Oh! Really. And, er, and how was that, exactly?"

With a disinterested shrug John jabbed his thumb over his shoulder. "Through the Striding Edge, of course. Molly Sigurdsson, pretending to be a maid, would find out which ship had the most stealable cargo, then she and the landlord, Michael, would arrange for their respective gangs to take their cut whenever they came through."

"Goodness. That was very clever of them."

"Yes, it was. It also explains why we never got robbed on our way north, when we were loaded down with what amounted to a load of scrap metal and glass, but on our way back, when we had great sack loads of cash with us."

"Yes, I suppose it does. Well, who'd have thought it. So there was no inside man after all. It was all because of the Striding Edge."

"Oh there was an inside man alright," said John. Mick suddenly became very still.

"What do you mean? What man? Didn't you just say—"

"That it was all down to Molly Sigurdsson. Yes, I did. But she had to be getting the information from somewhere."

"And, er, and where was that, do you think?"

"Simple, Mick. From you. She got her information from you."

"Me!" Mick squeaked, hurriedly dropping his voice back down to normal. "Me? What on earth makes you think I'm involved?"

"My suspicions were aroused when I saw you handing Miss Sigurdsson something by the back door of the inn. At first I thought maybe it was a token of your affection, that the two of you were polishing each other's brass work on the side."

Mick rose up in indignation. "I would never—"

John held up a hand to forestall the declaration of undying love that was clearly about to make an appearance. "But then I realised that it was information you were handing over. Information on when and where to catch the *Dragonfly* on her way back down south."

John could see Mick's mind racing.

"But it wasn't just us, was it?" he said, getting excited. "Everyone's been getting attacked. So what about the rest of them, eh? If I'm the one feeding her information, how am I meant to have known about all them as well?"

"Because it wasn't just you, of course. All the captains were in on it. That's why no one was very keen on me being involved in all this, and why none of you ever lost more than you could readily afford. You were paying your dues, letting yourselves get taxed so that you could stay in business. I figured that out from Captain Grant when she and I…" John waved his hands about in a suggestive manner, but Mick didn't understand. "Well anyway, she talks in her sleep, and what she said affirmed my suspicions, that the captains and the sky pirates had some kind of deal going. The only reason I think it was you and not Captain Tonbo is that she would never go for something like that. She's too honest. But you, an old navy man, a man of the world who knows his way around a dodgy port, you know that if you don't grease the wheels the whole thing will come tumbling down, right?"

John had a feeling he'd mixed his metaphors a bit, but he could tell by the look on Mick's face that he was right on the money. "You won't tell her, will you? She'd kill me if she ever found out. Please, I can't lose her. It would be the end of me."

"I won't tell her," said John. "Not now it's all over with." Mick breathed a sigh of relief. "But I tell you what, I know now why they call you Mick the Spanner, and it's not coz you're a mechanic, is it?" Mick's chin dropped to his chest. He looked like he wanted to cry.

On the other side of the pile of thatch, someone banged a wooden spoon on a metal pot. "Grubs up! Come and get it!"

John pushed himself to his feet. "Look, just no more lying from now on, eh? You've got a good thing going here, don't spoil it by doing anything dumb. Or dumber, should I say." Mick nodded glumly.

John followed his nose over to where the food was laid out, passing Billy along the way. He was sitting bent over his notebook, scribbling away with intense concentration. "Food's ready, y'know. Time to eat."

Billy snapped out of his spell. "Oh, yes. Right. Thank you. I'll be right there."

John's curiosity briefly overtook his hunger. "What's that you're writing anyway?"

"Poems, my friend. Simple poetry. A few words that, I hope, express the love and beauty I see all around me."

Billy held up his notebook for John to see. The handwriting was terrible but he could just about make out the words. "I wandered lonely as a cloud, that floats on high o'er vales and hills, when all at once I saw a crowd, a host, of golden daffodils."

"From our flight, do you see?"

"I do, yes. It's very good." John handed back the notebook.

"I hope one day to be published, then maybe others will feel inspired to come and see the beauty of the Lake District for themselves. We could make a real go of the Striding Edge, I reckon, if we can get a few more tourists in."

"Sounds like a plan," said John. "I look forward to seeing your name in print. Speaking of which, I never did get your last name. What is it? Billy what?"

"Wordsworth. And it's not Billy, it's William. William Wordsworth."

CHAPTER 10

...BUT NOT AWAYS

After a particularly awkward picnic with his sister and little Emily, during which John embarrassed both himself and Jane with his clumsy attempts to assure her that where she found love was simultaneously none of his business but also perfectly fine as far as he was concerned, John and Dexter arrived at the gates of Chard Mechanical intending to discover how Mr Shuttleworth was settling in as general manager. They instead found a large sign with red lettering hung above the factory gates which read, 'FOR SALE – ENQUIRE WITHIN.'

"Looks like Mr Shuttleworth's settling in quite nicely," said John.

"What the hell's he doing? He can't sell Chard Mechanical. That's, like, the entire company!"

"I'm sure he's not. Let's go see what he's up to before jumping to any conclusions."

The factory was busier than John and Dexter had seen it in a long time. The cobbled yard, with its piles of spare parts and raw materials, was full of men taking stock and reorganising everything. There were clipboards as far as the eye could see, and anyone not busy counting things or writing stuff down was busy carrying other things from where they were to where they ought to be.

The main building held one massive airliner nearing completion, another half-finished squeezed in next to it, and, from what they could hear, a third being put through its paces in the field out back.

"I thought this place was on its last legs," said John. "Did they get some big order in or something?"

"Good question," said Dexter, heading for the reception. "Let's find out."

In the reception they found Mrs Crabtree, the company's stalwart receptionist, dealing with a mountain of paperwork. "Mr Sinister. Welcome back. How nice to see you again." She said the words, she even smiled, but John felt the cold chill in the air.

"Good afternoon, Mrs Crabtree. How are you?"

"Busy, Mr Sinister. Very busy. This Mr Shuttleworth you found to run things is rather... full of ideas. He's got the whole place in an uproar."

"So I see. What's with the for sale sign out front?"

"I'm sure I've no idea. He hasn't felt the need to share such things with the likes of me, not officially by any road, so I wouldn't like to comment. I mean it's not like I've been sat at this desk for nigh on twenty year, come rain or shine, keeping this whole place going all on my lonesome. Oh no. It's not anything like that at all!"

"Um, okay. That's..." John pointed into the factory. "Is he in? Maybe I should speak with him directly."

"He is, but not in there. He's down in Mr Nomko's workshop." Mrs Crabtree locked eyes with Dexter. "Working on this new secret project of his."

Dexter shifted uncomfortably. They'd agreed to limit the number of people he would talk openly to for now, for fear of how some of them would react, but he was very tempted to tell Mrs Crabtree to go point her beady little eyes in another direction (and he would have too, if the shock might not have killed her stone dead on the spot).

"Right. Thank you, Mrs Crabtree," said John, ushering Dexter back outside before he did something John would regret. He had that look about him.

Nomko's workshop was a squat building next to the main factory, full of shelves and workbenches stacked high with failed prototypes and half-finished ideas. They found Nomko, the chief engineer of Chard Mechanical, giving what appeared to be a kettle with legs his full attention.

John tapped him on the shoulder and was greeted by a smiling Japanese face all covered in dirt and grease. "Mr Sinister! How wonderful to see you again."

"You too, Nomko. And I've told you, call me John."

"Of course, John. And Dexter, so good to see you too. How are you, Little One?" Nomko knelt down to scratch Dexter behind the ear, something only he was allowed to do.

"I'm good, thanks. All my bits in working order and all that."

"Good. Nomko is glad." He stood up again. "So, to what do we owe honour? Or is this social visit?"

"Actually we're here to see Mr Shuttleworth. Is he here?"

"Indeed he is! He has been most helpful. Mr Shuttleworth knows many thing about many thing. We have made much progress since he arrive."

"Progress? Progress on what?" asked Dexter.

Nomko winked knowingly. "You will see. Mr Shuttleworth. Mr Shuttleworth! We have guests."

With a clanging of tools, Mr Shuttleworth appeared from behind a canvas screen that had been hastily slung across the back of the workshop. "Ah! Mr Dexter, Mr Sinister. Good to see you again. How are you both?" He offered them each a greasy handshake.

"Fine, Mr Shuttleworth, thanks for asking," said John. "And you? How are you doing? Settling in okay, I see."

"Oh indeed I am. You were right, you know, I was in need of something new to sink my teeth into. I haven't felt this eager to put my boots on in the morning in years."

"So what's with the for sale sign outside?" asked Dexter. "You were asked to come down and whip this lot into shape, not sell it out from under us. And who gave you permission to do that anyway? I don't remember saying you could do that."

"Oh but you did, when you said I could do whatever I had to to put us in the black again."

"I didn't mean by selling up, for crying out loud! How can a company be profitable if you don't have a company anymore?"

"Relax," said Mr Shuttleworth. "I'm not selling all of it, just the airship side of things. Those things have been losing money hand over fist since day one. We'll be well shot of them."

"But the airships *are* Chard Mechanical. They're what we're known for. Without them, what are we? A company that makes omnibuses and metal doodads? That's not very... prestigious, is it?" In his flummoxed state, Dexter pronounced the word press-tidge-ee-us.

Mr Shuttleworth tapped the side of his nose, smiling. "Ah! Now that really is nothing to worry about. Nomko and I have been working on something. Something special, something unique, something that not only will make you a small fortune, but which will make Chard Mechanical a household name the world over."

Dexter's eyes narrowed. "Really? What?"

Mr Shuttleworth stuck two fingers in his mouth and whistled. There was a clatter behind the canvas screen, a thump as something heavy hit the floor, then a small, furry bundle of energy came scuttering out to say hello.

All floppy ears, wagging tail, and lolloping tongue, the little dog ran excitedly from one person to the next looking for someone to give it some attention. It very quickly settled on John, who was happy to provide it with head rubs in exchange for over-excited licks to the face.

"A dog?" said Dexter. "I don't get it. What are you going to do, start breeding them or something?"

The dog ran up to Dexter, a big dopey grin on its face. "Hello! My name is Doug. Will you be my friend?"

John didn't recognise all the words Dexter came out with as he fell over, but he understood their meaning well enough.

The End

ATTACK MARS!!

CHAPTER 1

Doctor Swann made her way along the phlogiston collection panels checking for the one thousandth time that each of their many collectors was connected up just as it should be. Every panel had been put through its paces over the past few weeks but tonight was the big one, tonight they were all going to be used at once, and she didn't want anything to go wrong.

Completing her circuit of the laboratory floor Dr Swann approached the vessel in the centre, at which all the phlogiston panels were pointed. An old diving bell they had gotten for a song because it wasn't entirely air tight anymore, there was really nothing there for her to check over. The diving bell was just somewhere safe for the test subject to sit whilst the experiment was ongoing. But she gave it a quick once over anyway, making sure that the seat inside was safe and secure, all its harnesses in place, and checking that none of the six springs that had been bolted around its base to cushion the device's landing (purely as a precaution you understand, the whole thing was perfectly safe) had fallen off since the last time she had checked a few hours ago.

Gazing up through the laboratory's great glass dome, Dr Swann considered the ever darkening sky. The skies were clear, and the stars were beginning to show, including the rather bright, slightly reddish one she had begun to see over the past couple of nights. She reminded herself, as she had done many times over the years, that she would have to get a book on the night sky, and learn the names of its many stars and constellations. It was a subject she had always thought on with great fascination, although not enough to do anything about it seemed.

There was no scientific reason that forced them to do their experimentations at night. It was an arrangement that had been agreed with the elders of the local village, after their first few daytime attempts had resulted in more than a few embarrassing 'accidents'. Quite why the light emitted by the phlogiston collectors made people feel the need to evacuate their bowels as quickly as possible Dr Swann didn't know. What she did know was, if the need arose, and said person found themselves not in easy reach of a suitable commode, that the evacuation would still occur whether said person wanted it to or not. Suffice to say there was more than one upstanding member of the community who had found their inability to sit down fast enough to be a little... soil-some, meaning their own standing in the community had gone downhill rather rapidly (as had much of their insides). Running the experiments at night was the best compromise they could come up with, the thinking being that anyone worthwhile would be at home in bed, with the curtains drawn, when they occurred, whereas those that were out and about after dark were up to no good and therefore deserved what was coming to them.

But even that hadn't been enough to make the local townsfolk look kindly on the 'so-called science monks'. These days the only person who didn't have anything bad to say about Dr Swann and her colleagues was Mr Iain B. Selwyn esq., the local baker. A well known sufferer of conniptions of the insides, the side effects of their experiments had given him a whole new lease of life. According to him he hadn't felt so free in years, so much so that he would undoubtably be sat on his outdoor toilet with the door open at that very moment, staring up at the night sky in eager anticipation of the kind of relief he had never gotten from decades use of Dr Sprogg's Innard Releaser.

Truth be told, Dr Swann preferred doing their experiments at night. The twinkling of the phlogiston collectors' spinning metal windmills in their little glass spheres as they cycled through every colour of the rainbow (and possibly a few others that had never been seen before) was quite mesmerising, even when observed through the smoked-glass goggles you had to wear to counter their other unfortunate side effect.

The laboratory door banged open and a man shuffled awkwardly into the room. He had cricket pads and gloves on over his brown robes, seat cushions tied all around his body, a battered pith helmet on his head, and a rather sour look upon his face. He was followed into the room by an elderly gentleman with an impressive beard. His robes had traces of egg down the front.

"Goodness! Mr Gibbett, you look very... well protected," said Dr Swann.

"I look a fool is what I look," said Mr Gibbett. "Are you sure all this is strictly necessary, professor?"

"Absolutely, Mr Gibbet. Absolutely," the old man replied. "One cannot be too careful in matters of scientific discovery. Do not fear the experiment that you do a thousand times, fear the experiment you only get to do once."

The professor chuckled heartily at his own joke, which made Dr Swann think it was another one from his old Oxbridge days. She smiled politely, because like all old jokes you had to have been there, and as a woman her chances of being at an Oxbridge college were slim to not bloody likely. "We're all set sir," she said, as the professor shuffled round the room inspecting things. "Everything is good to go."

"Excellent, Dr Swann. Excellent. On the ball as always." The professor gave one of the phlogiston collectors a minor adjustment. "Well then, no point in dilly-dallying is there. Shall we get started. Mr Gibbett, if you would be so kind." With a benign smile, the professor gestured invitingly to the modified diving bell.

Making his way clumsily up the metal ladder bolted to its side, the padded man squeezed into the bell through the little hatch at the top, landing on the chair within with an undignified plop. Grumbling to himself, he wriggled about as he tried to remember how the professor's insane strapping system was meant to work.

Dr Swann climbed up the ladder to close the hatch. "Best of luck, Mr Gibbett. I—" A seat cushion appeared through the hatch.

"Do something with this would you. I can't get the bloody straps closed with it on."

"Certainly," said Dr Swann, shoving the cushion under her arm. "Um, good luck. Again."

"What? Oh, yes. Yes. And to you too," said Mr Gibbett, managing a tight-lipped smile as the hatch door was sealed shut.

"Jolly good," said Professor Cray. "Now, the flywheel if you please, Dr Swann."

"Right away, sir," said Dr Swann, half saluting until she realised she still had a seat cushion in her hand.

There was a large metal disc bolted to the wall next to the laboratory door. It was connected to a number of gears, which in turn were connected to a couple of thick leather straps that ran up the wall and around the room. Pulling a lever to disconnect the gears, Dr Swann began laboriously turning the flywheel to build up momentum.

Pressing his face against against the small window in the side of the diving bell, Professor Cray waved to get Mr Gibbett's attention. "Remember now, you only need go a few feet in the air."

"I can go higher," said Mr Gibbett. "It's no problem, y'know."

Professor Cray shook his head. "No. This is about first principles. First we make sure that it works, then we worry about how far it can go. Understand?" Mr Gibbett nodded reluctantly. The professor smiled. Donning his tinted goggles, he indicated that Mr Gibbett should do the same. "How are we coming along," he called over to Dr Swann.

Dr Swann, quite red in the face, was having trouble keeping up with the flywheel. It had built up more than enough momentum for their needs. "We're good to go," she said, stepping back. "Just say the word, professor."

Professor Cray stepped out of the circle of phlogiston collectors. He nodded to Dr Swann, who took hold of the flywheel's gear lever. "Ready," he called. "And... ENGAGE!"

Dr Swann threw the lever and the drive mechanism sprang into life. All around the room momentum was turned into motion as, through an intricate set of straps and gears, a thousand tiny windmills began spinning within the confines of their little glass bulbs. At first they twinkled with reflected light, but then slowly, one by one, small glowing vortices began to appear, cycling randomly through the colours of the rainbow as they built in intensity. It was like someone had dropped a box of prisms on a bright sunny day, only more so. The effect was quite mesmerising; as was the sound. Besides the thrum of the flywheel and the clank of the gears, a low melodic hum was beginning to build, a strange tone that Dr Swann could only describe as like having the sun come up in your ear holes. It was utterly enchanting, astoundingly melodic, and better than any music she had ever heard before or since.

Dr Swann looked away, closing her eyes. She must not become enthralled again! She had a job to do. Nodding to Professor Cray, she gave Mr Gibbett a quick thumbs up. Gibbett gave a thumbs up in return, then he disappeared from view as he reached for a lever down by his feet. All around the room the pitch of the hum changed and the light began to oscillate, as slowly the heavy diving bell began to lift gently into the air.

Dr Swann clasped her hands together in glee. "It's working!" she exclaimed. "Professor, it's working."

Professor Cray nodded sagely as if to say, Of course it's working, I always knew it would. Then there was another change in pitch. The lights grew even brighter as the diving bell began vibrating violently in mid air. For a second Dr Swann thought she saw a beam of light shoot into the air, and then — POP! — the diving bell was gone. There was a sudden rush of air, the melodic hum vanished, and the lights of the phlogiston collectors quickly began to fade.

Dr Swann and Professor Cray stared at the empty space where the diving bell used to be. They looked at each other, then back at the empty space

"Where— Where is he, professor? Where's Mr Gibbett?" said Dr Swann.

"Um—," Professor Cray looked round the room. "Disengage the flywheel!" he ordered, marching forward. Dr Swann did just that. The sound of the gears faded to silence. Professor Cray inspected the dirt floor. Then he inspected the glass roof. It was intact, which was weird, because they'd had to remove part of it to get the diving bell in the laboratory in the first place.

"What do we do, professor? How do we get him back?"

Professor Cray ranged about the room, looking for answers. "Yes. Um... Get him back. Yes. Just so. We must do that."

"Yes but how!"

Professor Cray stopped and stared, a look of bewilderment on his face. "I... I don't know."

"Right," said Dr Swann. "Out of the circle. I'm firing her up again."

"But will that work?" said Professor Cray.

"No idea," said Dr Swann, spinning up the drifting flywheel with all her might. "But we have to do something." The second the flywheel was up to speed she threw the lever. The phlogiston collectors, replete with residual charge, came alive all at once.

Light and sound rippled around the room the same as before, yet somehow different. Before it had been more general, a casual building up of energy. This time it seemed directed somehow, like it, or something connected to it, had a purpose; like it knew what needed to be done.

Out the corner of her eye Dr Swann thought she saw the bright red star in the night sky flash briefly. She looked up in time to see the diving bell appear suddenly in the air ten feet above the laboratory roof. It dropped like a stone.

"Look out!" she yelled, ducking for cover.

The diving bell smashed through the lab roof, glass and metal flying everywhere. It slammed into the ground, its spring legs digging into the dirt, flinging it off to the side into a wall of phlogiston collectors. It bounced across the room, smashing another three panels before finally coming to a stop on its side somewhere near the dislodged flywheel and bent drive mechanism.

Dr Swann crawled out from under a fallen panel into a room full of dust. "Professor Cray! Professor Cray, are you alright?"

The professor stumbled through the dust towards her. "I'm alright, Dr Swann. Thank you." He looked to the battered diving bell. "You got him back. Well done. Quick thinking on your part."

"Let's not count our chickens yet, professor," said Dr Swann, picking her way through the broken glass. "Mr Gibbett? Mr Gibbett! Are you there, sir? Are you alright? Speak to me, Mr Gibbett. Please."

With an unhappy squeak the diving bell's hatch wheel turned slowly, its twisted metal giving way to whatever was inside's eagerness to get out. A clunk, and the hatch flew open, Mr Gibbett tumbling through onto the ground below. He'd lost his helmet and his gloves, and he had a bloody gash on his forehead that made the look of terror on his face that much more horrific to observe.

"Mr Gibbett! My God. What happened? Are you alright?

Mr Gibbett scrabbled about, wide-eyed and terrified. "Are they here? Did they come after me?"

"Who, Mr Gibbett? Did who come after you?"

"Them! Those— those— those things! With the skin and the eyes and the— the— the TEETH! My God, the teeth! There were so many of them. A whole army. Watching. Waiting. They tried to kill me. I barely got away. But they'll come after me, I know they will. They're coming after us all! It was— It was *an invasion*! Yes, that's what it was. They were about to invade. We must get ready. We must prepare. They could arrive at any minute. We must tell them. Tell them to prepare!"

"Them?" said Professor Cray "Them who?"

Mr Gibbett grasped the front of Professor Cray's robe. "EVERYONE!" he sobbed. "*Gah!!*" Thrusting a clawed hand desperately into the air, Mr Gibbett collapsed into unconsciousness on the laboratory floor.

"Goodness," said Professor Cray, smoothing down his robe. "What on earth was all that about?"

"No idea," said Dr Swann, looking up into the night sky. "No idea at all."

Notes From The Author

JOHN KENT - BRITAIN'S FIRST BLACK POLICEMAN

Whilst he was indeed a real person, John Kent (1805-1886) was never in fact a constable within the central Lake District. Thought to be the first black policeman in the British police force, he started his career as a parish constable in Maryport, before moving to Carlisle to become a supernumerary (later substantive) constable in 1837.

Known as "Black Kent" by the locals, he had a reputation as both a "quiet, inoffensive man" as well a "big and powerful" one. He was also a wily fellow. Whilst arresting two 'coiners' (counterfeiters) he handcuffed one to the fire grate of his own home before going to arrest the other, leaving an unloaded pistol with his wife, Mary, with instructions to shoot the prisoner if he tried to escape.

Kent was dismissed from the Carlisle constabulary in 1844, be-coming a court bailiff and then a parish constable in the Eskdale ward. He later returned to Carlisle where, at age 78, he was recorded in the census as being a railway attendant in the Citadel Station waiting rooms.

Kent died at his home in 1886, with the local paper the *Carlisle Patriot* describing his passing as "The Death of a Carlisle Notable".

If you'd like to know more about John Kent I recommend reading 'Britain's First Black Policeman – The Life of John Kent, A Police Officer in Cumberland 1835-1846' by Ray Greenhow (published by Bookcase).

https://www.bookscumbria.com/product/cumbrian-books/history/britain-s-first-black-policeman/

DEAR READER

I'd like to thank you for giving The Dragonfly Deliver Company a try. I hope you've had fun reading it, and if nothing else have been entertained by the second outing of Hammermsyth's most famous detecting agents. I'd also like to thank everyone who read my first book, Dexter & Sinister: Detecting Agents, and decided to come back for more. I appreciate you more than you could possibly know.

If you have a moment to leave a review for The Dragonfly Delivery Company it would be very helpful to me. The more people who go on Amazon or Goodreads to leave a review, the more likely I will be able to bring out future Hammersmyth Tales for you to enjoy.

Book three, ATTACK MARS!!, will be out as soon as is humanly possible. It promises an expansion of the world of Hammersmyth, with new characters, new technologies, and new ways for people to mess things up, all in the name of Science and Progress. Oh, and there may be aliens. Or will there? Who knows. It's a distinct possibility. Either way, you'll have to read it to know for sure!

Thank you again, and if you really have enjoyed The Dragonfly Delivery Company then please do tell your friends.

About the Author

Born in the north of England, a stones throw from the Lake District, Keith studied film making at university before moving to London to work in film and TV. After twenty years of doing other people's bidding he went around the world, trained as a yoga teacher, rode a camel, and was finally able to publish his first novel, something he has dreamed of since he was eight years old, when he asked for a typewriter for Christmas.

Currently residing in Leeds, when he's not up a mountain Keith can be found trying to get his foot behind his head. He hasn't managed it yet, but he'll get there one day.

www.keithwdickinson.com

ACKNOWLEDGEMENTS

My utmost thanks go out to my readers Paul D and Annalisa W, whose feedback has been invaluable as always, with special thanks to my brother Paul who suggested the character of Fenris Wolf, giving the whole story the shape it has today. A good villain makes all the difference. And thanks to my editor, Jess Lawrence, who helped make that story shape not only recognisable, but legible, comprehensible, and properly punctuated.

Thanks too to my patient illustrator Mike Smith, for bringing the Dragonfly to life, and to my designer Nell Wood, for another excellent cover design. They say that with food the first bite is with the eye, and so it is with books. If the cover of The Dragonfly Delivery Company has made you hungry to see what was inside, it is entirely down to these two lovely people.

And a special thanks to my friend, the author Matt Wainwright, who is always willing to offer an opinion on whatever literary quandary I may have, no matter how trivial (even if I ignore him completely and do something else instead). Cheers mate.

www.jesslawrence.com

www.facebook.com/doodlebagsillustrations

www.nellwood.co.uk